PLAYING WITH TROUBLE

A BROTHER'S BEST FRIEND ROMANCE

PLAYING
BOOK 4

LAINEY DAVIS

Cover by Qamber Designs.

Editing by Becky and Leah with Bookcase Media.

Audiobook narration by Alastair Haynesbridge and Charlotte North.

Audio engineering by Kyle Gaffney.

CHAPTER 1
HOWIE

What am I even doing with my life?

I'm a professional athlete living in my best friend Rookie's condo, taking turns as designated driver on drinking holidays. I'm the sober one on New Year's Day because I ate Rookie's beef jerky and had to chauffeur him as punishment. And so…I'm on airport duty for his sister.

I honestly don't know if he'd actually kick me out if I refused to get Baby Rookie from her flight, but I'm also too irritated to deal with finding a realtor, and I really don't feel like living in a hotel.

It's bad enough living in a hotel on the road with the Pittsburgh Fury men's hockey team.

I turn the volume down on the stereo in my G-Wagon and concentrate on merging on Pittsburgh's weirdest bridge. I swear, I will never understand the Fort Pitt tunnel entrance as long as I live here.

Which might not be much longer if I don't get my shit together. But my hockey career is a problem for later. Right now, I have to move four lanes to my left without barfing when I check my blind spots, and then I have to find Ella Rujkowski—Baby Rookie—and bring her back to our place.

I didn't mean to stay up all night. We started things off

right, with a casual hang at the meatball joint, just me and my main buds. But then someone suggested a club a few blocks away and, well, here we are. I'm not hungover, but I'm groggy and dehydrated for sure.

At least it's easy to find a parking spot at the airport on New Year's Day. I grab a hat, smash my hair over my forehead, and adjust my sunglasses, ready to find Rookie's kid sister at baggage claim.

I should probably have gotten her cell or something. I doubt Rookie will respond to a text or answer a call. I'm not even sure what flight she's on, but I guess there aren't too many coming in from Minnesota this morning.

I wedge myself into a seat near the baggage carousel, too tired to even mess around on my phone while I wait. I haven't seen Ella in years. Not since Rookie and I went to college, when she stopped being a permanent fixture in the carpool for all our tournaments and practices.

The Rujkowskis invite me and my parents to hang with them in the summers, but I'm never really in the mood to see my parents, so here we are.

How different could Ella look, though? I close my eyes and think back…imagining Rookie's face on a girl with braids. She always wore glasses and seemed pissed off. I guess I would be pissed off if I had to tag along in a car full of hockey gear and hockey guys, and I didn't play the sport.

A few passengers appear on the escalator, but none look familiar. My phone buzzes in my lap, and I grab it quickly, but it's just a message from my dad hoping I make a "statement" in the new year. I snooze the conversation, not wanting to see his flood of unsolicited advice based on his glory days as the league's meanest enforcer.

So far, nobody seems to recognize me, but I don't see anyone who might be Ella either. I scrub a hand down my face and lean forward, scanning the terminal.

Through the haze of my headache and dehydration, I

notice a super hot chick bent over to tie her shoe. She's thick in all the right places—someone who wouldn't break with a guy my size on top of her.

The barely-liquid blood in my veins surges directly to my pants as I let myself stare at this woman's incredible backside. I want to knead my fingers in it and squeeze. I want to feel those plush thighs around my waist, bury my face between those tits, and feel every inch of this woman's softness against my body.

Damn, she's fine. Her dark jeans fit her perfectly, and she's wearing bright pink sneakers with a purple sweater of some kind. It's got a V-shaped neckline that has me wanting to go on a search-and-rescue mission down the front. I watch her bite a glossy, plump lip and glance around. She's looking for someone.

Someone gets to take her home. Lucky bastard.

I'm all-out staring now, masked by my mirror sunglasses, watching her heft a giant bag off the belt. I should probably offer to help her. Be a hero.

I'm about to stand up and do it, I swear, when she turns and looks directly at me, striding across the space like she's on a mission. I glance around, and there is nobody else over here on this bank of seats.

I grin and sit back, feeling the arms of the chair dig into my thighs. The world just isn't built for guys who are six-three and weigh two-twenty, so I adjust myself and plant my grin back on my face before I notice that she is not amused.

She grunts and drops the handle of her suitcase, which tips over with a clatter that squeezes my brain cells. I wince, and she scolds, "Seriously? He sent you?"

I clear my throat. "I'm sorry?"

She snaps her fingers in my face. "Hello? Bernard? Where is my brother?"

A horrifying realization begins to settle into my aching body. This sexy goddess is not a stranger at all. This is the girl who used to wipe peanut butter hands on my pants in the back seat of Jason Rujkowski's parents' Jeep while hockey sticks jabbed us both in the back of the head.

This kid—who is in fact the sexiest woman I've ever seen—is Ella Rujkowski.

I'm sitting here half hard, ogling my roommate's kid sister.

I CLOCKED BERNARD HOUSER FROM THE TOP OF THE ESCALATOR and felt immediate annoyance at seeing him again. And then I realized he was here alone, without my brother, and my entire life as an afterthought in the Rujkowski family came rushing back to the surface.

Of course, Jason's offer to help me find my feet was just another empty promise. Whatever. At least Bernard can lift my bag.

I pout alongside him as he hefts the giant monstrosity upright and grabs the handle with his thick, hockey-roughened fingers. I haven't seen him in years, but I recognized the huge frame and curly hair sticking out from his black hat.

"Rookie, I mean Jason, asked me to grab you so he could finish cleaning for you," he lies, and the effort is just charming enough that I inhale, smile, and gesture toward the sliding doors.

"Right. Great. Thank you for picking me up."

I clutch my purse against my sweater, and Bernard pauses, scratching the back of his neck, the motion hitching up his hoodie and revealing a glimpse of taut muscle above the waistband of his sweatpants. Thankfully, those are black, so I'm not flagrantly staring at his junk, but it's bad enough that I'm noticing the added muscle and bulk that Bernard "Howie" Houser has put on since I last saw him at a college hockey game my freshman year.

He and my brother both got drafted and left college early for the pros, and I thought that might give me a blessed taste of anonymity for my last few years, but Minnesotans never forget a hockey star.

Even in clinical rotations, I was Baby Rookie instead of Ella, under the spotlight of my brother's fame. At least I'm used to it. It seems like Jason's name is the only way I get in doors professionally with grades like mine. The only nurse extern jobs I managed to find were in my hometown—no thank you—and here in Pittsburgh, where my brother's stupid face is all over billboards promoting beef jerky.

"Ella?" Bernard's voice cuts through my thought cloud, and I realize he asked me something.

"Sorry. What?"

"I said, don't you want a jacket or something? It's like five degrees outside."

I arch a brow at him, and he laughs, shaking his head and rolling my bag through the doorway toward the parking garage. I follow, absolutely not noticing the tight, round bulge of his gluteus maximus, deciding not to chastise him for asking a Minnesota girl if she's cold.

He makes his way toward an expensive SUV, clicks a key fob that opens the hatch, and tosses my bag inside like it weighs little more than a rancid hockey glove.

I head toward the passenger seat, surprised to find him sprinting around the car to open the door for me. Judging by the look on his face, he, too, is taken aback by his chivalrous instinct. "Thanks," I tell him, climbing into the ridiculously luxurious leather seat, eyeing the heated seat button as soon as he turns the engine on.

This is a major upgrade from my last experience sharing a ride with Bernard Houser, that's for sure.

He turns the radio down to a quiet hum and backs out of the parking spot, tossing his arm around the back of my seat despite the backup camera that would have guided him just fine. I'm hit with a wave of spicy deodorant and soap, and I really shouldn't find it ... there is really no word apart from titillating. Shit.

"So," I flick on the seat warmer, eager to distract myself from unclean thoughts. "What's the tea on the team? Who does Jason want to punch?"

Bernard chuckles and leans a bit to check his mirrors. God, he's a good driver. Ew, why am I focused on that? He says, "Your brother and I are tight with the Stag twins. You know Tucker and Alder?"

I shrug. Of course, I know my brother's teammates, but I'm not going to let this douche canoe know that I follow the Fury. I'm here to forge my own path.

Bernard's fingers drum on the steering wheel, knuckles scarred and forever bruised from his trade. "Well, Tuck knocked up our goalie's ex-wife, and they have twins. So that's been ..."

I whistle. "Awkward! Wait. Isn't the goalie also a Stag?"

Bernard shakes his head, glides into the passing lane, and zooms by a battered Buick struggling to keep pace on the highway. "We have a tandem goalie rotation. Grentley is the one with the ex-wife. Gunnar Stag is absolutely in love with his wife, and I'm pretty sure it's mutual."

Neither of us has much to say in response to that, so I stare at the window as we ease past an IKEA. "Tell me about my brother's place. Is he still hoarding meat and being weird about sharing?"

Bernard grunts, which seems like a neutral response to questions about my brother's juvenile rules. "Let's just say we do our own food shopping."

"Good to know. Good to know." I turn to face Bernard. "You still live there, too, right?"

He turns and stares at me, slowing the car until someone behind him lays on the horn. He snaps his eyes back to the road and speeds back up, saying, "When you say *too*, do you mean … did Rookie … are you staying at our place?"

"Well, yeah." I cross my arms over my chest and stare at him as he tries not to look at me, following signs toward downtown. "Jason told me to come stay with you guys until I pass my NCLEX and get hired permanently. What's the issue?"

I watch the muscles of Bernard's throat as he swallows, glancing over his left shoulder and heading into a tunnel. "There are only two bedrooms in our place," he says, drumming those fingers on the steering wheel.

The car shoots out of the mouth of the tunnel, revealing the city of Pittsburgh in a yellow splash of beauty and bridges. The city makes an entrance as profound as the realization that my brother has once again fucked up my life.

I came here as a probationary hire, with the promise that my wealthy-ass brother would help me out while I study for my boards. "Did he…there's no bedroom?"

Bernard shakes his head. "I thought he got you a hotel room or something."

I don't say anything else as we drive north, toward a giant brick building with an old HEINZ sign on the roof. Bernard parks his SUV in silence and walks around to the back to get my bag. I climb down and follow him to the lobby of a very fancy building, with exposed brick and round windows. A ketchup factory reimagined as luxury condos.

I cling to a small kernel of hope that my brother rented me an entire apartment above his or something, that he doesn't expect me to spend multiple months sleeping on his couch while he and Bernard come in and out at all hours from their infamous orgies.

I stare at the floor in the elevator, follow Bernard down the hall, and pause inside the doorway as he yells, "Yo,

Rookie. We're here." At the echoing silence, Bernard sighs. He rolls my bag to the corner, props it against the wall, and then starts pounding on a door down the hall while I take in the view from the floor-to-ceiling windows in the living room.

The guys have no curtains or anything, and the morning light streams through. I take in the white leather sofa, which seems comfortable enough for a night, but faces the river, where even on New Year's Day, a fleet of barges and tugboats blasts horns as they push coal west toward my hometown. Toward a place that really has no better options for me than this.

My brother emerges half-clothed, clearly hungover. "Ellie belly!" He sees me and spreads his arms for a hug. I frown. "What? No love for your bro-bro? Come here, kid."

He starts to walk toward me, and I hold out a palm to stop him. "You told me I could stay here while I pass my boards."

He leans on the wall next to me. "Yeah. Welcome home. You know the rules." He winks at this, like it's funny.

Thankfully, he reads the room and his face shifts. "Look, Ella, this is a ten-thousand-dollar couch. It's not like we have an air mattress for you. What's the issue?"

I gesture toward the window. "Where am I supposed to change? Where do I put things? You don't even have shelves."

He shrugs, as if all of this is minor. "You can change in the bathroom. What's the big deal?"

I look at the couch. No blankets. I glance down the hall, where there's just one other door, presumably to Bernard's room. "So am I showering in your bathroom? When you're in there with a puck bunny?"

His face shifts. "Of course not. You'll use..." My brother's words freeze on his tongue as he finally grasps that he is sending me to the edges of his lifelong cardinal rule. Every team he's played for, every elite roster I had to observe as a passenger in the background of his life, has been serenaded with the famous Rookie Rules:

Don't wear my gear, don't eat my food, don't touch my sister.

I stare at my brother's bloodshot eyes, willing myself not to cry. I will not cry in front of him. The last time I did that—when I got my first period in the bleachers of his hockey tryout and bled through my pants, and he threw a fit about lending me clothes—he was unbearable afterward for months. He treated me like I was a baby with brittle bones and demanded I keep a bag of necessities in the car at all times. Of course, the hatch was filled to the brim with his gear and Bernard's, so that bag and all my homework and on-the-go meals had to be wedged by my feet, which were already smooshed from Bernard's manspreading in the back seat.

No.

I am not going to cry right now.

"She can have my room," a voice utters—Bernard's.

"What?" My brother and I turn in unison to stare.

He shrugs. "She needs privacy. She can sleep in my room. I'll knock before I hit the head."

I close my eyes, not sure what to do with the gratitude I feel for this small kindness. When I gather my wits, I smile at my new roommate. "Thank you, Bernard. I will find someplace else to stay as soon as I can."

Jason rumbles some sort of noise. "Suit yourselves," he says, and turns on his heel back into his own room.

Bernard lifts my suitcase and pushes it through the other door. "I'll just grab one of the pillows and let you get situated," he says.

He pauses at the foot of the massive bed that takes up most of the room. "I'll change the sheets, too. We have laundry in the kitchen."

I duck into the bathroom as he yanks on the linens, closing the door and staring at myself in the mirror. I'm a ball of test anxiety, who barely passed my coursework, with a provisional job in the emergency department at the trauma center where my brother's face shines down from a billboard onto my place of employment.

I'm squatting in another man's bedroom, standing in his bathroom that still carries the faint scent of body wash, the air still damp from the shower he clearly took before coming to get me at the airport.

I don't want to think of Bernard as a hero. But I'm feeling something unfamiliar as I stare at his bath towel hanging neatly on the hook. Maybe a nap will bring me some clarity.

When I open the bathroom door, I'm alone in the bedroom, which has been made up with fresh sheets, the comforter tossed neatly over the one remaining pillow in the center of the bed. I collapse onto it face down and fall asleep, worried about these confusing feelings I'm having toward my brother's best friend.

CHAPTER 3
HOWIE

I don't even know if Ella came out of my room to eat yesterday. I tried to nap on the couch, ended up at Gianna's Meatball Joint with a bunch of the guys, and spent a sleepless night with streetlights shining in my face while my feet dangled off the end of a sofa so firm I think I dislocated a hip.

I have to get ready for morning skate now, and I need to get a bunch of shit from my room.

I peel a banana, trying extra hard to listen and see if Ella is moving around in there. I tap gently on the door, crack it open in the silence, and see that she's not here.

The bed is made, and her suitcase in the corner is unzipped, neat piles of clothing and stuff arranged tidily along the wall. I guess she snuck out like a panther to go to work or something.

I grab my gear and a protein shake from the fridge, listening for Rookie, who starts his morning hacking right on cue. Eventually, he emerges phlegm-free from his room and starts eating his precious caveman meat. I often forget how serious he is about people touching his stuff, but in the end, most hockey players are neurotic about shit they think might impact their game.

I should have known better than to eat his jerky sticks,

and I definitely know better than to interrupt his game-day flow. "You ready?" I gesture at the key rack, knowing we will take his car to morning skate, come home to nap, and then take my car to the arena for the game itself. Routine is essential.

I'm quiet on the way up to the practice facility, mostly because I'm exhausted and sore, but a thought occurs to me as Rookie flips on his headlights entering the highway. "Hey, man, we need to get some curtains or something in the living room."

He looks at me, confused. "Why?"

"Well, for one thing, it's weird that people can see in if we're hanging out, right?" He shrugs. Rookie knows he's hot, and he knows people—women—like to look at him. "But also, bro, I had streetlights burning holes in my eyes all night. Are you good if I call someone about installing some blinds or something?"

He scrunches up his face. "I guess it's your money. Nothing permanent, okay? I don't know how long I'll hang on to this place."

"I don't think window treatments are going to impact your property value, Rook."

He laughs. "Look at you with the lingo. Your ma still doing real estate over in St. Paul?"

I shrug. I haven't talked to my parents in a bit. I know there's basically no money left from my dad's career, and I know they had some big feelings about investing in mine. I sent them my signing bonus, and they barely acknowledged it.

I don't know what they're doing with their time these days. Probably better that way.

We pull through security at the rink and go through our morning skate routines. Today's Grentley's day in goal, and he has that beef with the Stag twins on defense, which means there's tension.

Coach gives me a look while I wait for the line change, and I see he's expecting me to lighten the mood or something, but I don't know if I have it in me. Best I can come up with is to ask Rookie, "Is your sister coming tonight?"

I know what it means to phrase it that way, and it draws the response I'm expecting. "Don't talk about my fucking sister."

Cappy nudges Rookie with his shoulder. "Chill, man. I assume Howie meant, 'Will she be at the game?' Let me know, and I'll make sure Essence has her number."

This starts a cascade of guys asking about Ella moving to town, hanging out with the Partners and Wives, and Rookie's confession that he didn't get Ella a ticket or mention the game to her.

"What the fuck, man? You are such a jerk sometimes."

We skate through a few plays, bang the rust off, and switch lines. I tap gloves with Tucker Stag as he glides onto the ice. His falling-out with Grentley really has been a thing with the whole team. Lots of guys feel the residual tension in ripples.

Back on the bench, Rookie sits by Cappy. "I didn't think about her coming to games. She has to study for some test at her job. I'll ask her about tickets, okay?"

"Do that." Our captain bops Rookie on the helmet with his gloved fist.

We finish morning skate and head home for mandated naps. And it's weird, because my bed is right there, and if Ella is at work, she won't need it until well after I'm on the ice.

But I sort of told her she could have the room.

I flop onto the couch and manage to drift off despite the sun glare from the river.

———

I wake to the smell of smoked meat. When I open my eyes, Rookie is standing over me, a jerky slim dangling from his mouth like a cigarette. "What's with you? We have to leave in ten minutes."

He spins on his heel, and I know he's off to find a very precise set of socks and boxer briefs. I struggle to care about my own game-day socks. I splash cold water on my face at the kitchen sink and grab my keys, driving us both to the arena while blaring our death metal playlist.

And then we get our asses handed to us by Boston.

———

I should go home and crash. I know this. But fucking Grentley commented on half the team being frat guys with no self-control, and the rebel in me cannot let him be right.

So, how do I demonstrate my professionalism and commitment to winning?

I drive straight to Gianna's, order a bucket of meatballs, and pound a bucket of beers alongside the protein.

I'm not the only one. Spinner and Rookie have a similar supper. They also have jersey chasers draped over them. Gianna usually keeps the riffraff out so we can eat in peace, but I think those guys found some bunnies waiting for autographs after the game and brought them along.

With my remaining sliver of consciousness, I look around the room lit softly by Edison bulbs. The farmhouse-wood tables and benches are mostly empty at this hour. I'm alone in a corner with the dregs of my Michelob and teriyaki balls, and Rookie looks like he's about to round third base with each hand at another table.

My thoughts drift to Ella, whether she found anything for dinner, whether Rookie will force her to pay penance if she raids the fridge, or give her grace because she's his sister.

I laugh out loud at that, causing Gianna to pop her head

out from the swinging door to the kitchen. "You alive over there, Howie?"

I nod, my head sloshing a bit. "Yeah. But I think I should head out."

She extends her palm. "Give me your keys. I'll get the dishwashers to take your wagon home again."

I hand her my fob and a few hundreds for the pair of high school kids who, I realize, have made a decent side hustle from transporting my car for me each time I get wasted.

Gianna pats my hand, and I head outside, the frigid wind biting through my dress shirt. I probably spilled sauce on myself. I manage to hail a silver taxi and mumble my address before falling asleep in the back seat.

Between the lack of sleep, the loss, the heat of shame at my bad habits, and my concern for a woman I shouldn't think about at all, I am a mess. When I get to the building, without my keys, I don't even have to explain myself to the doorman. I shuffle behind him to the elevator and down the hall, sliding him more money when he unlocks the condo and bids me goodnight.

Shedding the pieces of my suit as I walk, I stumble into my bedroom, onto my bed, and pass the fuck out.

CHAPTER 4
ELLA

There's a hand on my boob.

I come slowly to wakefulness, feeling warm and squeezed all over. I realize there is a human hand on my boob.

There's also the weight of an arm across my waist and a wall of heat pressed against my back, solid. Firm.

I notice the faint rhythm of someone breathing against the top of my spine.

I hold my breath, assessing.

The arm around me tightens, pulling me closer, and a low sound rumbles from behind me—half groan, half exhale—directly into the curve of my neck. My entire nervous system lights up like a trauma bay.

Bernard is in bed with me. I can smell beer and garlic, and underneath it, that same body wash from his bathroom, the one that hung in the damp air when I first walked in here yesterday. Bernard Houser is wrapped around me like I'm a body pillow, and his peen is unmistakably, aggressively hard against my backside.

I should elbow him in the ribs and launch myself out of this bed. I should do literally anything other than what I'm doing, which is lying perfectly still with my heart hammering while Bernard shifts in his sleep and presses closer, his fingers splaying across my stomach through my thin sleep shirt.

His hand is enormous. It covers the entirety of my breast and, oh my lord, he's stroking my nipple. He makes that sound again—God, a low moan that vibrates through my bones. I feel something pull tight and hot between my hips.

Nobody has ever held me like this. Not because I'm unwantable. I've been told I'm pretty. I've been asked out. But every one of those would-be boyfriends was either trying to get close to my famous brother or scared off by him. Jason literally beat up the guy who asked me to prom, and then I went to the same university where he was even more famous.

So no. Nobody has held me like this. Like I'm something to pull closer.

I press my lips together and stare at the wall, trying to steady my breathing. My pulse is doing something medically inadvisable. Bernard mumbles, releases my boob, his thumb tracing a slow, tantalizing arc across my stomach, and I make a noise I will deny to my grave.

I need to get out of this bed. I need to wake him up. But my body is a traitor, and every time I try to shift away, his arm tightens, or he hums against my neck, or his hips press forward, and the cycle of absolute insanity repeats itself.

Fine. Enough.

I grab his wrist and lift his arm, scooting forward on the mattress. The movement does what my internal screaming could not—Bernard goes rigid behind me. There's a beat of silence so absolute I can hear the barges on the river outside.

Then: "Oh, fuck."

The mattress lurches. Bernard throws himself backward so hard the headboard cracks against the wall, and something crashes off the nightstand—a glass of water, maybe, or his phone. I roll over in time to see him standing at the foot of the bed in black boxer briefs, chest heaving, eyes wild in the dim light, and even in the chaos of this moment, I cannot help but notice that Bernard Houser's body is a medical marvel.

He's massive, built like a damn Viking. He has a broad chest, dense shoulders, and a solid slab of an abdomen. My gaze slides down, and I cannot look away from the protrusion at his crotch.

"Ella." His voice is wrecked. "I am so sorry. I forgot...I didn't...I was at Gianna's, and we lost the game, and I had too much to drink, and I forgot you were—fuck. I am so sorry."

He drags both hands through his curls, pacing two steps in the small space between the bed and the bathroom door. He's tripping over his own suit pants, crumpled on the floor alongside a dress shirt that appears to have brown sauce on it. I see it now. The guys lost, went out for gross food, and he probably drank an entire pitcher or three of alcohol.

He scrubs his face with both hands. "I owe you, Ella. I'm so sorry."

He lingers in the doorway, outlined by the faint light from the living room windows. I can see the mortification radiating off him. He opens his mouth, closes it, and then says again, "I owe you," before disappearing into the bathroom.

I hear the lock click. The fan turns on. The shower starts.

I lie on my back and stare at the ceiling and try to convince myself that my heart rate is elevated purely from the adrenaline of being startled awake. This is a normal physiological response to an unexpected stimulus. Tachycardia. Vasocongestion. Elevated cortisol.

Completely standard.

Except my hand drifts to my stomach, to the place where his palm was, and I can still feel the phantom weight of it. I can still feel the press of him against my back. The sound he made.

I roll onto my side and curl my knees up, pressing my thighs together.

The shower runs. I think about Bernard in there, and then

I try very hard not to think about Bernard in there, and then I think about him anyway.

I can imagine the water sluicing over those shoulders, those hands braced against the tile. I wonder if he's thinking about what just happened, whether he's—

I press my face into the pillow.

Which smells like him. This whole room smells like him, like soap and something woodsy and, now, beer and garlic and regret.

I owe you, Ella.

The words sit in the dark room like an offering. I know it's a learned response to my brother's absurd transactional friendship requirements. Bernard doesn't owe me a thing after offering me the use of his bed and room and simply forgetting about it one night.

My brain spirals through yesterday's events. My first shift at Mercy was twelve hours of controlled panic. I wrestled new systems, new faces, a charge nurse who looked at my badge and said "Oh, Rookie's sister?" before I'd even clocked in.

I was assigned to a senior nurse named Susan, who talks too fast, calls everyone "honey," and told me I'd "figure it out" when I asked where the supply closet was. I stood in the hallway of the ER holding a blood draw kit and feeling like a complete fraud while an attending yelled at someone behind curtain three.

And then I came back here, exhausted and wired and questioning my life choices. I managed to study like three flashcards for my boards before I passed out. I didn't even wake up when Bernard slumped in here. I have about five more minutes before my alarm and my second shift at Mercy.

I lie in the dark listening to my brother's best friend shower, and I feel more alive in my body than I have in months.

The water turns off and I squeeze my eyes shut as he leaves the bathroom.

I hear him move down the hall. The couch creaks. Silence.

I owe you, Ella.

Here is the thing about being a twenty-three-year-old virgin: it's not a badge of honor, and it's not a source of shame. It's just a logistical reality, like not having a driver's license until you got to college because your parents were too busy driving your brother to practice to take you to the DMV.

It's a thing that didn't happen because there was never space for it.

But I'm almost a real adult now. I have a job—provisional, terrifying, but mine. I spent two weeks filling out paperwork and watching videos about regulatory details I immediately forgot. I have a test to pass that will determine the entire trajectory of my professional life. I have roughly ten thousand problems stacked on top of each other, and somewhere near the bottom of that pile, beneath the NCLEX and the apartment search and the question of whether I'll ever feel like a real nurse, is the matter of my persistent, inconvenient virginity.

I can't exactly swipe through dating apps while crashing at my brother's place, the hockey player. I can't bring anyone home. I don't know anyone in this city except my brother and his teammates, so my options are limited to approximately zero.

Except.

Bernard is not dreadful to look at. This fact has been abundantly clear to me over the past forty-eight hours.

Bernard, given the party-boy reputation that precedes him and the approximately nine hundred women I've seen tagged in his social media over the years, is probably very skilled at sex.

Bernard, as of three minutes ago, owes me a favor.

This is a terrible idea. I know that asking my brother's

roommate to take my virginity is the kind of decision that belongs in a cautionary tale, not a life plan.

But I'm lying here in his bed, in his sheets, and I can still feel his hand on my nipple, and I think: what if I just got it over with? What if I claimed this one thing for myself? One less obstacle between me and being a fully formed adult who doesn't flinch when someone touches her because the sensation is so foreign it short-circuits her brain?

I owe you, Ella.

I let the idea sit in the dark, testing its weight, the way you press a bruise to gauge how much it hurts.

I'll ask him. Not now, obviously, with him reeking of beer and regret. But soon.

In the meantime, I have to get back to the hospital. I've got to be standing by Susan by seven on the dot to usher in gunshot wounds and burn victims galore.

I slide out of bed and gather my scrubs from the neat pile by my suitcase, pulling them on in the dark. I brush my teeth, lace up my shoes, grab my badge, and my bag.

I slip out the front door without a sound. The hallway is quiet. The elevator hums.

I step into the cold Pittsburgh pre-dawn and walk toward the bus stop, feeling the ghost of Bernard's erection with every step.

CHAPTER 5
ELLA

A kid comes in on a stretcher before Susan and I can even start a conversation. The paramedics seem confident he's a lost cause.

A certainty builds inside me, though. I will not lose this kid.

He's maybe nineteen, hit by a car crossing Penn Avenue, and his abdomen is rigid and distended while the EMTs rattle off vitals that paint a grim picture.

I hear all the words from my clinicals, from exams I failed. But today their meaning resonates. Tachycardic. Hypotensive. Altered consciousness. Internal bleeding, almost certainly, and he needs blood before he needs anything else.

"O neg, two units, now," Susan calls out, and I'm already moving.

This is the thing about me that doesn't make sense on paper. I can't pass a multiple-choice test to save my life. I transpose numbers. I second-guess written answers until I've erased holes through the Scantron. But put me in a room with a patient who is actively dying, and my hands are steady, my mind is clear, and I know exactly what to do.

I grab the blood from the rapid infuser, check the unit number against the patient's band twice, because shortcuts kill people, and spike the bag while another nurse named Aarthi preps the second line.

She's fast. I noticed that about her yesterday: precise hands, no wasted movement, and a face that gives away nothing even when things are bad. She's new like me, but I haven't had a chance to talk to her.

"Pressure's dropping," McKenzie says from the monitor. The third nurse in my hiring class has her fingers on the kid's radial pulse, and her voice is steady, but I can see her jaw tighten.

She's from Louisville and has a drawl that comes out when she's stressed, which means every word right now has about four syllables.

"Squeeze the bag," Susan tells me, and I'm already squeezing it, forcing the donated blood in as fast as gravity and my grip will allow. The kid's skin is gray. His eyes are half-open, and seeing nothing.

The attending materializes and starts calling for imaging, surgical consult, the whole cascade that happens when someone's belly is full of blood. I stay focused on my line, on the flow rate, on the kid's face. I watch his color. I watch his breathing.

"Second unit's ready," Aarthi says beside me, and we swap bags without a word, like we've been doing this together for years instead of two shifts.

It takes eleven minutes. The surgical team takes him upstairs with enough volume on board to keep his pressure stable, and the attending pauses at the nurses' station to look at our little trio of new hires.

"Good work in there," Dr. Reed says, and he's looking at me when he says it.

Susan squeezes my shoulder on her way past. "Quick hands, honey. Real quick."

I nod, wash my hands for the third time, and feel absolutely nothing about the compliment because I was just doing the obvious thing.

Aarthi finds me restocking the supply cart twenty minutes later. "You were a machine in there," she says, leaning against the counter with a coffee cup that says WORLD'S OKAYEST DOCTOR, which she claims she bought to annoy her parents. "Was that your first spleen situation?"

"I just handed them blood."

"You handed them blood at the exact right speed with zero hesitation while a teenager was dying. That's not nothing, Ella."

I shrug, because I don't know what to do with praise that contradicts the running narrative in my head. The narrative says I'm the one who graduated late, the one who can't test, the one whose biggest accomplishment is being related to a hockey player. The narrative is very loud.

McKenzie appears with a coffee from the vending machine. "Y'all. I need to decompress. That child's mama is in the waiting room, and I almost lost it."

We huddle by the supply cart, three new hires in identical scrubs, drinking terrible coffee in the fluorescent purgatory of Mercy Hospital's emergency department. McKenzie tells us about her first code back in Louisville—she cried in the bathroom for twenty minutes, and when she came out, her preceptor handed her a biscuit and said, "Now do it again."

Aarthi tells us her mother called during her lunch break yesterday to remind her that her cousin Priya had just been accepted to Johns Hopkins Medical School.

"My brother's face is on the vending machine," I offer, and they both stare at me.

"I'm sorry, what?" McKenzie turns to look at the vending machine in question, where Jason's face is indeed grinning from a beef jerky advertisement plastered to the side panel. "Oh, my GOD. That's Rookie from the Fury? Rookie is your BROTHER?"

"Unfortunately."

Aarthi snorts. "So that's why Susan called you Baby Rookie on your first day."

"I will pay you both actual money to never call me that."

"How much money?" Aarthi asks. "Because my student loans would like a word."

This is nice. This is something I haven't had in a long time—maybe ever. Friends who see me as Ella, not as Jason's tagalong. They know I'm good in a trauma bay, they know I drink my coffee black, and they know I have student loans that match theirs. For the first time since arriving in Pittsburgh, I feel like a person instead of an appendage.

———

Around four, the ER hits a lull that Susan says is unusual. McKenzie is charting. Aarthi is restocking. I pull out my phone and open the NCLEX practice app, figuring I can squeeze in a quiz while things are quiet.

The first question is about fluid resuscitation in hemorrhagic shock.

I literally just did this. I just did this with my hands, in real time, on a real human being who is currently alive because of the blood I pushed into his veins.

The question asks me to identify the correct order of interventions from a list of four options. I read them. I read them again. The words blur and rearrange themselves. Option B and Option C look identical to me. I know—I KNOW—the answer, but the way it's written on the screen doesn't match the way it lives in my brain, and I second-guess myself, change my answer, and get it wrong.

I try fifteen more questions. I get nine of them wrong.

The app cheerfully informs me that my score falls below the passing threshold and suggests I "review foundational concepts." I close the app and shove my phone in my pocket and stand there for a moment in the hallway where, a few hours ago, I helped save a life.

I can do the work. I just can't pass the test about the work.

The rest of my shift passes in the blur of a busy ER. I help with a dislocated shoulder, two lacerations, and a woman having a panic attack who just needs someone to sit with her and breathe.

That's an easy one for me. I hang with her and complain about my brother, and she laughs at my jokes. But I don't think there's a multiple-choice question about this bedside manner.

I clock out at seven, change in the locker room, and think about my route home. It's a two-mile walk or a 40-minute bus ride with multiple transfers.

The January sky is gray-black and heavy, so I decide to split the difference and walk to the 67 stop, boarding a bus that smells like wet wool and old piss.

I lean my head against the window, watching Pittsburgh scroll past, and feel the exhaustion settling into my bones like concrete.

When I let myself into the apartment, it's quiet. I glance to the left and see Jason's door is closed, which means he's either asleep or not here. I can't remember if they had a game today. The living room is dim, lit only by the television, playing a low-volume sports highlight show. There's no head sticking up above the back of the couch, but as I step further into the room I see Bernard is lying there.

He's in sweatpants and a T-shirt that strains across his chest, with an ice pack balanced on his hip. He looks up when I come in and makes a face that might be a smile if it weren't laced with residual mortification.

"Hey," he says carefully.

"Hey."

I am instantly reminded of the feel of his erection against my ass and of my plan to cash in on his offered favor.

My stomach growls. Loudly.

I glare toward the kitchen, mentally cataloging the contents of the fridge and calculating what punishment my brother would cook up if I curbed my hunger with his stash of special food.

My brother's caveman diet is sacred territory, and I'd sooner poke a bear than touch his elk cubes or whatever artisanal protein he's hoarding this week.

"There's meatballs in the fridge," Bernard says, reading my dilemma. "I brought back extra from Gianna's. Help yourself."

"Seriously?"

"Yeah, of course. They're mine, not his. Top shelf, red container."

I find the container and dump a generous portion into a bowl. I'm too tired and hungry to care how it might look for a plump girl like me to be wolfing down a giant bowl of meatballs.

Bernard has already felt what I've got going on here. But I do plan to ask him to undress me and plunder my lady-cave...

The microwave hums while I grab a fork and glance back toward the living room, where Bernard is trying to adjust his ice pack without moving too much.

"Hang on," I tell him.

I go to the freezer and pull out a fresh one. At least these guys seem to stock the good ice packs.

"Yours looks done." I swap the melted pack for the fresh one, positioning it properly against his hip flexor without thinking. "Did you stretch after your skate?"

He blinks up at me. "No?"

"Stretch after your skate, Bernard."

"Yes, ma'am."

The microwave beeps. I retrieve my meatballs, which smell obscene—garlic and basil —slow-cooked beef in a tomato sauce that makes me want to weep. I settle into the armchair across from him, and eat three meatballs in rapid succession before I'm capable of human speech.

"These are incredible."

"Gianna's the best. That's our spot—me and the guys. She takes care of us." He shifts on the couch, winces, then repositions the ice pack. "How was work?"

"Good. Hard. I helped with a trauma case."

"Yeah?" He's watching me with an expression I can't quite read. Like he's not sure where the conversational landmines are. "Was it intense?"

"A kid got hit by a car, ruptured an organ. We got blood into him fast enough for surgery."

I say it plainly, and Bernard stares at me. "Jesus, Ella."

"It's the job."

"That's a hell of a job."

I eat another meatball. He watches the TV. The silence between us is different than before. It's warmer somehow, less loaded. Or maybe more loaded, but in a different direction. I'm aware of his body on the couch, the bare feet pointed toward me, the way the television light catches the curve of his bicep. I'm aware that twelve hours ago, that arm was wrapped around my chest.

"How was it with Grentley and Tucker last night?" I keep thinking about how awkward that must feel for the team dynamics. But I have no idea what led to the first guy's divorce.

Bernard grunts. "Tuck's babies were there. I think the actual babies make it all less ..." He drifts off without naming the team mood.

"Twins are brutal. I'm sure everyone sees that."

He nods. "Yeah. Anyway, we lost."

"Bummer." I finish my food and set the bowl on the

ottoman. I look at Bernard Houser, who is pretending to watch a hockey highlight reel and absolutely not succeeding at acting chill.

"So," I say. "About that favor you owe me."

His head turns. I watch the wariness settle into his features. "Yeah. About that. Listen, I really am—"

"I don't want an apology."

"Okay." He shifts upright on the couch, the ice pack sliding. "What do you want? Name it."

I take a breath. I rehearsed this approximately forty-seven times during my shift—in the supply closet, on the bus, in the elevator—and it still feels unhinged when it leaves my mouth.

"I want you to deflower me."

The silence that follows is so complete I can hear the gel in his ice pack shifting.

Bernard's mouth opens. Closes. Opens again. He looks like a man who has just been told something in a language he doesn't speak and is trying to translate it in real time. His eyes dart to Jason's closed door and back to me.

"You—" He stops. Swallows. "I'm sorry, I thought you were going to ask me for a ride to work or something."

I hold his gaze. I don't blink.

He runs a hand through his curls, staring at me like I just defibrillated him without warning. Then something else crosses his face—a different kind of alarm.

"Wait," he says. "How DO you get to work?"

"I take the bus."

"The bus."

Bernard sits fully upright, the ice pack falling to the floor forgotten. "You're taking a public bus in the dark. Early in the fucking morning. To a trauma hospital."

"That is correct."

"In Pittsburgh. In January."

"Bernard, I work in an emergency department. I see worse

things inside the building than anything that happens at a bus stop."

"That is not comforting, Ella."

"I haven't even been exposed to hepatitis yet. And I've had all my shots."

He looks at me like I told him hockey was canceled. Like the concept of a woman voluntarily riding public transit to a job where teenagers arrive spurting blood is more alarming to him than the fact that I just asked him to take my virginity, which, I realize, he has not actually responded to.

"Bernard."

"Yeah?"

"Did you hear what I said?"

He opens his mouth. Nothing comes out.

I pick up my bowl, carry it to the kitchen, and rinse it in the sink. "If you owe me, then that's what I want," I tell him over my shoulder, then walk down the hall to his bedroom— my bedroom, temporarily—and close the door.

CHAPTER 6
HOWIE

I AM EITHER CONCUSSED AS FUCK, OR ELLA RUJKOWSKI JUST asked me to "deflower" her.

Baby Rookie asked me to put my penis in her vagina, stood up, rinsed her bowl, told me to think about it, and waltzed into her room as casually as if she'd asked me for a ride to work.

Which, what the fuck. She should not be taking the bus to that part of town in the dark.

My brain throbs, and the blood circles my crotch as I try to make sense of the world right now. Should I go wake up Jason and tell him what I probably hallucinated?

I want you to deflower me.

I press the heels of my hands into my eyes and try to think about literally anything else—forechecking strategy. Penalty kill rotations. The trajectory of a puck off the—nope, I'm thinking about Ella's mouth forming the word "deflower" again.

Here's the thing: every instinct I have says yes. I've wanted her since the airport, when I didn't even know it was her. I was hard against her this morning, and I'm half hard now on this stupid couch just from the memory of her voice, steady and clinical, laying out her proposition between bites of Gianna's meatballs.

But she said it like it would be a task. Like picking up dry cleaning. Like I'm a service provider, and she's got a coupon.

And that—I shift on the couch, staring at the ceiling where the streetlights paint long yellow streaks—that's what's messing with me. The reality of Ella's situation lines up for me like coach's notes on the whiteboard.

Nobody helps her with anything. Ever.

She's fresh out of college in a new city, taking the damn bus to work at nightmare o'clock in the morning in January. How did she even know what bus to take? I have no clue how to ride the bus, now that I think about it.

Does Jason know any of this? Or is he too busy monitoring his lucky shoulder pads?

It dawns on me that Ella Rujkowski has been solving her own problems in the margins of other people's lives since she was a kid in the back of that SUV.

I told her I owe her, and maybe I owe her more than I thought when I said it.

———

I'm standing in the kitchen with my keys in my hand when she comes out of my bedroom in scrubs, hair pulled back, badge clipped to her pocket. She's got a bag over one shoulder, and she's moving quietly, clearly trying not to wake anyone.

She stops when she sees me.

"What are you doing?"

"Driving you to work."

"Bernard, you don't have to—"

"Get in the car, Ella."

She stares at me for a second. I watch her run the calculation—argue with me, or get a warm ride to work instead of standing at a bus stop in the dark. Practicality wins.

The G-Wagon is freezing when we climb in, but I started it remotely from across the parking garage, so the heated seats are already cooking by the time we get inside. Ella sinks into the leather and lets out a tiny, involuntary sigh of satisfaction that goes straight through me like a blade. I grip the steering wheel and focus on backing out of the parking spot.

We drive in silence for a few blocks. The city is dark and empty, just us and delivery trucks and the occasional bus lumbering along its route. The one she'd be standing in the cold waiting for right now.

She doesn't bring up "the question." I don't either. But the air in the car is different—heavier, charged—and I'm aware of her in the passenger seat the way you're aware of a bruised rib when you're sitting still.

She's got no makeup on. Her scrubs are Oxford blue. She looks like someone who saves lives for a living, because she does, and I have no business being this attracted to a woman in hospital-issued polyester.

I pull up to the entrance at Mercy, and she unclips her seatbelt. "Thank you, Bernard."

"I'll pick you up after your shift. What time?"

"That's not necess—"

"What time, Ella?"

She presses her lips together. I think she's trying not to smile. "Seven-thirty."

"I'll be here."

She climbs out, hoists her bag, and walks toward the entrance. Two other women in scrubs are converging from different directions—one of them Indian with a low ponytail, the other one white with a high ponytail. They spot Ella, and there's a chorus of greetings, a group hug right there on the sidewalk, the three of them laughing about something as they push through the doors together.

I sit in the drop-off lane, watch the doors close behind them, and feel something ease. She has friends. She's building something here that has nothing to do with Jason, hockey, or me.

I should connect her with Cam, Essence, and some of the other partners and wives. That's the kind of thing Jason should have thought of—introducing his sister to the people who could make Pittsburgh feel like home. But Jason didn't think of it, because Jason doesn't think about Ella. It sucks to realize this, but my best friend and roommate thinks about Ella the way you think about furniture you've had so long you don't notice it anymore.

I drive to practice with the passenger seat still warm.

———

I'm first on the ice, which never happens. I skate laps until my lungs burn and my hip screams at me, and I'm still going when the guys start filtering in.

Spinner hops the boards and glides up beside me, matching my pace. "You look like hammered shit, Howie."

"Didn't sleep great."

"The couch thing? Dude, just tell Rookie's sister to get a hotel."

"She's fine. I'm fine. The couch is fine."

"You just said fine three times, which means everything is shit." Spinner bumps my shoulder with his. "Let's get meatballs later. Gianna's got a new sauce."

I'm about to tease Spinner about Gianna when Mayhem materializes, six-foot-five and silent, smelling like a hockey sock. He says nothing. He just skates alongside me for a few strides, looks at my face, and says, "You good?"

"Yeah, man. I'm good."

He holds my gaze for half a second longer than comfortable, nods once, and skates away. That's Mayhem. He doesn't need you to talk. He just needs you to know he noticed.

Coach blows the whistle, and we run drills. Rookie shows up exactly on time, already jawing with Cappy about some play from the last game. He doesn't ask about Ella. He doesn't ask if she got to work okay. He doesn't ask if she ate, slept, or is adjusting to the city.

He asks me to pass the tape.

I bite my tongue so hard I taste metal. There's a version of me that grabs Rookie by the collar right now and says *your sister saved a kid's life yesterday and took a bus home in the dark and you didn't even get her a game ticket, you absolute walnut.* But that conversation is coming. Not yet. Not here.

We scrimmage. I play like garbage—too distracted, always a half-step behind. Coach gives me a look. I give him nothing back.

———

I'm in the Mercy parking lot at 7:21 p.m. with the seat warmer on and my head against the headrest. I almost fall asleep, but then I see Ella pushing through the doors, shoulders tight with exhaustion, and I sit up and unlock the car.

She slides in. "You actually came back."

"I said I would."

That sound again—the small sigh as the heated seat hits her back. I am going to hear that sigh in my dreams.

We drive for a few blocks before she says, "So."

"So."

"Have you thought about it?"

I have thought about nothing else for the past eighteen hours, but sure, let's be casual. I turn onto the bridge and choose my words, which is not typically something I bother to do.

"I'm not doing it as a favor," I say.

I feel her stiffen in the seat beside me. "Okay—"

"Hang on. Let me finish." I check my mirror, merge, and buy myself a few seconds. "You asked me like you're checking something off a list. And I get why—you're practical, you've got a million things going on, you want to handle this efficiently."

"What's wrong with efficiency?"

"Nothing. Except this isn't a blood draw, Ella."

She's quiet. I can feel her looking at me.

"Here's what I think," I say, and I'm building this argument in real time, which is dangerous, but I've never been great at planning. "You deserve to know what you're doing. Not just the first time—like, all of it. You should feel confident. You should know what you like, what works for you, so that when you meet the right guy..."

"The right guy," she repeats flatly.

"...you're not fumbling through it. You shouldn't have to figure it out with someone who doesn't know what he's doing, or someone who doesn't give a shit whether you enjoy it." I pause. "You're right that I know what I'm doing. And I give a shit."

The silence in the car is enormous. I chance a glance at her. She's staring at me with an expression I can't decode.

"So you're proposing, what, exactly? A lecture series?"

"I'm saying I'll teach you. Just like I would teach you if you asked me how to change a tire. Because I want you to have a good experience, and because—well, you know what you look like, Ella."

"I know nothing," she says, and there's something complicated in her voice.

"You look like someone I have to try very hard not to stare at." The words are out before I can vet them. I keep my eyes on the road. "So if you want this, I'm in. But I'm not collecting on a debt. That's not what this is."

She's quiet for long enough that I start to panic. Then she says, "Okay."

"Okay?"

"Okay, Bernard. You can tutor me. In sex."

I exhale. I might be concussed. I am almost certainly unwell. "Good. Great. And listen, I can help you study for your boards, too. I'm good at that kind of stuff."

She laughs, and it's the first real laugh I've heard from her—sharp and surprised, as I shook it loose. "You want to tutor me for the NCLEX."

"Why not? I've been quizzed by every trainer, PT, and team doctor in the league. I know shit. Supraspinatus, infraspinatus, teres minor, subscapularis." I tick them off on my fingers, steering with my knee for a second.

"Did you just steer with your knee?"

"Focus on the muscles, Ella."

She's smiling. I can see it from the corner of my eye—a real smile, not the tight, polite thing she gives Jason. "Fine," she says as I pull into the parking garage. "You can tutor me. For both things. But not tonight. I've been on my feet for thirteen hours, and I smell like a hospital."

"You smell fine."

"I smell like betadine and someone else's blood."

"Okay, that's fair."

She gathers her bag and opens the door. We ride the elevator up to the condo in silence, and I unlock the front door, gesturing for her to enter first. "Thank you for the rides. Both of them. I mean… the driving. To work." She closes her eyes briefly. "I'm going to bed."

"Goodnight, Ella."

She disappears down the hall, and the door clicks shut.

I lie on the couch and stare at the ceiling and wonder what the hell trouble I just signed up for.

CHAPTER 7
ELLA

FOR THREE DAYS AFTER OUR AWKWARD CONVERSATION, NOTHING happens with Bernard "Howie" Houser. When I pass him in the living room, he shouts out questions about shoulder muscles. I respond with accuracy. We smile.

He is awake and dressed when I emerge on work days, and drives me to the hospital in his fancy-ass car, quizzing me about body parts he knows. He peppers his trivia questions with anecdotes like "I shredded my polar plates when I blocked a shot sophomore year of high school," or "that was the time your brother destroyed his temporalis. Remember when he couldn't chew?"

Neither of us brings up the other tutoring, the sex lessons that keep me up staring at the ceiling with anxiety.

I'm off today, and using my time wisely: lying in Bernard's bed in sweatpants and a hoodie, surrounded by textbooks, failing a practice quiz on my phone. It would go easier on a laptop, I think, but my brother said no to my request to borrow his, and I don't have one.

My family wasn't ever destitute, but getting Jason to the pros was a significant financial investment, and it never really occurred to my parents to save anything for me. I didn't want to add a computer to my loan burden when there was a perfectly good lab full of them at school. I guess that was short-sighted.

A tap on the door pulls me from the cardiovascular system and my financial pickle. Bernard pokes his head in. "Ella? Can I grab some stuff real quick?"

I glance at the clock. It's not quite ten, but they must have had a short practice. Or maybe they have a game today. I haven't kept up. "Yeah. Of course. Come in."

Bernard edges the door open and pauses at the sight of me buried in textbooks. He's in jeans and a Henley with the sleeves shoved up his forearms, which are extremely muscular, a detail I absolutely do not need right now. "Studying?"

"Dying."

"That bad?"

I hold up my phone and show him the score: 54%. He winces. "The questions are asking me to identify the symptoms and treatments of different M.I.'s."

He grabs a hoodie from the closet and leans against the doorframe. "Have you eaten?"

"I had coffee."

"That's not food. Come with me to Gianna's and fuel up. You can study there."

I rest a hand on my stomach, which growls at his mention of Gianna's food. "Fine."

Gianna's Meatball Joint is a fifteen-minute walk from the apartment, tucked into a block of converted row houses with a faded hand-painted sign above the door. Inside, it's warm and smells like garlic and delicious, savory food, looking all cottage-core with rustic wood and fancy old lighting.

"They're not really open yet, but Gianna lets the Fury come whenever." Bernard walks in like he owns the place, which, based on how much money he probably spends here, he functionally might. A woman about our age with dark hair piled on top of her head emerges from the kitchen and points a wooden spoon at him.

"Howie. Sit. You want the usual?"

"Please. And whatever she wants." He gestures at me. "Gianna, this is Rookie's baby sister. Ella."

Gianna turns her attention to me and does a full scan. Her eyes move quickly, the way another woman sizes you up when you show up with a man she knows well. "*This* is the baby sister?"

"Ella," I say, extending my hand.

She shakes it. Firm grip, calloused palms. "You caused quite a stir with Thing 1 and Thing 2."

I roll my eyes, liking her description of my brother and his lifelong best friend. "Yeah, well, most of that is due to Jason being an idiot."

"Mm-hm." She looks at Bernard with an odd expression. "Your usual plus a meatball sub for the lady. Sit down."

We take a corner table, and I spread my books out while Bernard gets us water from the metal carafe. It's quiet—too early for the lunch rush, too late for breakfast. The restaurant is empty except for a kitchen worker unstacking chairs and the distant clatter of pans.

"Okay," Bernard says, pulling my review book toward him. "Cardiac symptoms. Walk me through it."

I stare at him. "Right now?"

"You've got the book. I've got nowhere to be. Rookie's doing photos for the beef jerky people until like four." He flips to the chapter on cardiac electrophysiology and turns the book to face me. "SA node. Go."

I take a breath. "The sinoatrial node generates the impulse. It's the pacemaker. Sends the signal through the atria—"

"Which contract?"

He talks me through the whole thing, and I'm surprised when the answers flow from my mind readily. I'm not even distracted or anxious. Bernard grins. "See? You just nailed it."

I stare at him. I did just nail it. The same sequence I scrambled on my phone this morning came out clean and in order.

"It's easier when you ask me," I say, and the realization sits funny in my tummy. "On the test, the words get jumbled. The options all look the same. But when someone asks me out loud, I just ... know it."

"Then we do it out loud." He says this like it's obvious, like the solution to my lifelong testing problem is simply Bernard Houser asking the questions. "Every morning, every night. We quiz until you can do it in your sleep."

Gianna appears with two plates: a mountain of meatballs in red sauce for him, a sub overflowing with the same for me. She sets Bernard's down and raises an eyebrow. "Look at you hydrating responsibly."

"It's ten thirty, Gianna."

"That's never stopped you before." She pats his shoulder and disappears.

I frown at the space. "She really doesn't mind if you come in before lunch?"

Bernard has his mouth full already. He chews a bit and says, behind his fist, "She comes in early to prep catering orders and such."

I bite into the sub and almost groan. The meatball is perfect—tender, garlicky, the sauce rich and tangy against the crusty bread. Bernard watches me eat with an expression of open satisfaction, like feeding me is a personal accomplishment.

"Okay," I say, after swallowing. "I have a question that's not about cardiac conduction."

He picks up a meatball with his fork. "Shoot."

"When do we start the other lessons?"

Bernard's fork freezes halfway to his mouth. A flush crawls up his neck—actual, visible red—and he glances toward the kitchen, then the door, then back at me. "Maybe not the best place to discuss the, uh, curriculum."

"Nobody's here, Bernard."

"Gianna has ears like a bat."

"I'm not proposing we do it on the table. I'm asking when."

He puts the fork down. The flush has reached his ears. This enormous, confident hockey player who has reportedly slept with half of Pittsburgh's fangirls is blushing at the mere mention of sex with me. I find this deeply satisfying.

"Today," he says, and his voice drops. "If you want. Rookie's out until four."

The meatball sub suddenly requires all of my attention. I take a very deliberate bite and chew slowly, aware that my own face is doing something I can't control. "That works."

We finish lunch in a state of heightened awareness. Every time our fingers brush, reaching for napkins, I feel it in my spine. He pays the check, and I don't argue because I am saving all my argumentative energy for other things.

The walk back to the apartment feels like three hours. The elevator ride is silent. He unlocks the door. The apartment is empty, quiet except for the fridge humming and a barge horn from the river.

Bernard closes the door behind us and stands in the entryway, suddenly looking less like a confident sex tutor and more like a man who has realized he agreed to teach a woman about intimacy and maybe didn't think through the logistics.

"So," he says.

"So."

"Do you want to… should we… the couch?"

"Not your bed?"

"That's your room right now. I don't want you to feel like I'm—it should be somewhere neutral. Where you're not sleeping." He rubs the back of his neck. "The couch is neutral."

I sit down on the ten-thousand-dollar leather monstrosity. It's enormous, wide enough for both of us, deep enough to lie down. I understand now why Jason spent this much on a sofa. It's the size of a small country.

Bernard perches beside me, leaving a careful gap. He

angles his body toward mine, and I'm struck by how large he is this close. The breadth of his shoulders, the thickness of his thighs, the way his hands rest on his knees like he's not sure what to do with them.

"Okay," he says. "So. First thing. Tell me what you've done before."

"Done?"

"Kissing, touching, whatever. So I know where to start."

I consider lying. Inflating my experience into something less humiliating. But Ella Rujkowski didn't survive nursing clinicals by bullshitting her assessments, so I tell the truth.

"I've been kissed. Four times, by three different people. Two of them were terrible. One was at a party, and I think he was trying to reach my tonsils. The third was nice, but we were interrupted by my brother threatening to disembowel him."

Bernard closes his eyes briefly. "Of course he did."

"I've never been touched. Below the neck, I mean. Or above the knee. I've never—" I stop. Regroup. "I haven't done anything, Bernard. That's the whole point."

He doesn't flinch. He doesn't look pitying, surprised, or excited. He just nods, like I've told him my blood type. Like he's the triage nurse and this is information he needs to do his job well.

"Can I touch you?" he asks.

"That's why we're here."

"I know. But I'm asking."

Something shifts in my veins. "Yes."

He moves closer, eliminating the gap between us. His right hand comes up, and I brace for—I don't know what. Something aggressive, maybe. Something that matches his reputation.

Instead, his fingertips brush my jaw.

Just that. The pads of his fingers, tracing the line of my jaw from my chin to the soft spot below my ear. His touch is so light I almost can't feel it, and yet my entire body responds, a wave of heat that starts where his skin meets mine and spreads downward.

"Breathe," he says quietly.

I realize I've stopped. I inhale, and he smiles—a small, private thing—and his fingers trail down. Along the side of my neck. Over the ridge of my collarbone, left to right, slow and deliberate, following the bone like he's memorizing its shape.

"Clavicle," I whisper, because apparently my brain defaults to anatomy when it's short-circuiting.

"Good girl. What's it connected to?"

Fuck me, my nipples are hard at the sound of Bernard Houser calling me a *good girl*.

"The..." His thumb traces the hollow of my throat, and I lose the word. "The scapula. And the sternum."

"Mm-hm." His fingers drift along my collarbone to my shoulder, where the neckline of my hoodie stops him. He doesn't push past it. He just traces the edge, fingertips following the fabric line, and I realize he's mapping the boundary between clothed and not-clothed without crossing it.

"You're staying on top of the clothes," I say.

"For now. Yeah."

"Why?"

"Because you've only been kissed, Ella. We're not going from that to naked today."

This is so reasonable it irritates me. I want to argue—I'm an adult, I can handle it—but I also recognize the logic. Start with the basics. Build competency before advancing. It's how I learned to start an IV, and it's probably how I should learn this.

"Fine. Can I touch you, too?"

"Anywhere you want."

"Where do men like to be touched?"

He laughs, a real one, surprised out of him. "I mean, the obvious answer is our dicks."

"I'm aware."

"But the real answer is anywhere. If it's someone you want touching you, it all feels good." He takes my hand and places it on his chest, palm flat against the Henley. I can feel his heartbeat, fast and hard. Not as calm as he's pretending to be. "See? Just that. Your hand is right there. That's... yeah."

I spread my fingers against the cotton. His heat radiates through the fabric. I can feel the contour of his pectoral muscle, the ridge of his sternum, and beneath it all, that rapid heartbeat that tells me my brother's best friend is not remotely as composed as his voice suggests.

I move my hand up, over his collarbone, and along the side of his neck. His pulse jumps under my fingertips. I reach his jaw, roughened with stubble, and he holds perfectly still, barely breathing.

I trace his eyebrow. There's a scar there, a thin line through the hair where it doesn't grow back, the kind you get from a high stick or an elbow. My finger follows it, and Bernard's eyes close.

"When did you get this?"

"Juniors. Kid caught me with a stick in the eye. Eight stitches."

I touch the scar again, gently, and his breath stutters. Without planning to, I slide my fingers into his hair. It's thick and soft, curls wrapping around my knuckles, and when I drag my nails lightly across his scalp, he makes a sound that I recognize. The same low groan from the other night. The one from when he was pressed against me in the dark.

My whole body flushes.

"Ella." His voice is rough.

"Is this okay?"

"This is very okay. This is...you should know that if you

keep doing that, I'm going to...it's just, my body is going to react, and I don't want you to..."

"Bernard."

"Yeah?"

"I'm a nurse. I understand physiological responses."

He exhales something that's almost a laugh, and I keep my fingers in his hair, scratching gently, and I feel it—the shift of his hips, the subtle press of his thigh against mine as he adjusts, and the unmistakable evidence that Bernard Houser is aroused. Hard against my hip. Just like the other night, except this time we're both awake, both choosing this, both here on purpose.

I don't pull away. He doesn't pull away. We sit like that on the stupidly expensive couch, my fingers in his hair, his hand resting carefully on my collarbone, and it feels nothing like tutoring. It feels like standing at the edge of something very high and deciding whether to jump.

His face is close. I can see the gold flecks in his brown eyes, the scar in his eyebrow, the way his pupils have blown wide. He's looking at my mouth. I'm looking at his.

"Can I kiss you?" he asks.

"Yes."

He leans in. His hand slides from my collarbone to the back of my neck, cradling my head, and his mouth meets mine. It's slow. It's warm. His lips are incredibly soft and plump, like pillows pressed gently against mine. It's nothing like the kisses that came before, no aggression, no tonsil excavation, no fumbling. Bernard kisses me like he has all day and intends to use every minute of it. His stubble scrapes my chin, and when his tongue touches mine, I make a sound that I couldn't suppress if my life depended on it.

He pulls back just enough to look at me. "Good?"

"Yeah. Really good. But am I doing okay? I don't know what to—"

He kisses me again. Deeper this time, one hand in my hair,

the other braced on the couch beside my hip. I grip his Henley with both fists, and my back arches toward him, and I can hear myself making sounds that I should be embarrassed about, but I'm not, because Bernard makes a sound right back every time I pull him closer.

I don't know how long we stay like that, kissing on the couch, fully clothed, his hands never straying below my collarbone, mine tangled in his hair. I realize we are lying down side by side, pressed together from chest to knee, his leg wedged between mine, my fingers tracing the scar in his eyebrow over and over because it makes his breath catch every time. His hand is on my waist, over the hoodie, and I can feel every finger like a safety belt. And I can feel *him*, hard against my thigh, and neither of us pretends it's not happening.

He kisses the spot below my ear—the one his fingers found earlier, the one that makes my spine dissolve—when we both hear it.

Keys in the lock.

We separate so fast that I nearly roll off the couch. Bernard is on his feet in one fluid motion, crossing to the kitchen like he's been standing there the whole time. I grab the nearest textbook and open it to a random page, sit upright, pull my hoodie straight, and try to slow my breathing from its current rate of "patient hyperventilating."

Jason pushes through the door, smelling like processed meat and hair product. "Hey. What are you guys doing?"

"Studying," I say, holding up the textbook. It's upside down. I flip it.

"I'm quizzing her," Bernard adds from the kitchen, where he's opened the refrigerator and rummages inside.

"Nerds." Jason drops his bag and heads for his room. "Don't drink my shakes. I need a shower."

His door closes. The water starts.

I look at Bernard. His hair is wrecked. His face is flushed.

His Henley is stretched where I grabbed it. He looks at me, and I look at him, and we both start to laugh—silently, shoulders shaking, because Jason is twelve feet away and has no idea that his best friend and his sister were just tangled together for sex lessons.

"I give you an A," Bernard whispers, and he chugs my brother's green smoothie mixture while we both laugh until our ribs ache.

CHAPTER 8
HOWIE

TODAY'S GAME DAY DRIVE TO THE ARENA FEELS DIFFERENT AS I SIT stewing beside Rookie, death metal cranking.

I know why I feel off. I'm one thousand percent aware that Ella will be taking the bus home from Mercy Hospital after dark, alone, and her brother either doesn't know or doesn't care.

I adjust my tie in the rearview as I sit at a light, spying the fans already lined up for security. Rookie sits beside me, thumbing his phone and chewing the hell out of a piece of mint gum.

"Hey," I say, merging onto the road. "Can you text Ella and make sure she takes a cab home tonight? And that you'll pay for it? I don't want her walking around Uptown in the dark."

Jason snorts without looking up. "She's fine, dude. She's been getting herself around since she got here."

"She works in a trauma center, Rook. She sees what happens to people walking around alone at night."

"Ella's tough. She's from Minnesota. This is barely cold." He locks his phone and shoves it in his pocket. "Besides, she's a big girl. She can handle herself."

Something about the way he says "big girl" — careless,

almost dismissive — hits me in a way I wasn't expecting. I keep my eyes on the road.

"Speaking of roommates," Jason says, shifting in his seat, "you owe me a smoothie. That was my last bag of protein greens, and I know you drank one the other day because I weigh that shit."

"I'll buy you more greens."

"It's not about buying more. It's about the rules, Howie. My stuff is my stuff. I let Ella stay, I let you have the couch situation, but the fridge is…"

"You *let* Ella stay," I repeat.

"Yeah. I did. She needed help, and I stepped up."

The words sound like a puck to the glass—jarring, violent. I feel my hands tighten on the steering wheel. I should let it go. I should nod, change the subject, turn up the music, and focus on the prep.

But I've never been smart. I'm the guy who says yes to everything, and I'm about to say something I can't take back.

"You stepped up," I say. "You offered her a couch in a room with no curtains. You didn't pick her up from the airport. You didn't get her a game ticket. You don't know what bus she takes to work, or what time her shift starts, or that she saved a kid's life her second day on the job."

The silence in the car is enormous.

"She takes two buses, actually," I continue, and I can hear my voice getting harder. "At five in the morning. In the dark. In January. To a trauma center where people come in with stab wounds and overdoses and internal bleeding, and she stands there, and she handles it, and then she gets on the bus and comes home and studies for the most important test of her career on her phone because you wouldn't lend her your laptop."

"She can use the—"

"You said no, Jason. She asked, and you said no. Because

of your rules. Your stuff, your food, your fridge, your smoothie."

Rookie's jaw is tight. He's staring straight ahead. "She never said any of that to me."

"Because she never asks for anything! That's the whole problem!" I smack the steering wheel, and the horn blares. A pedestrian jumps, and I mouth "sorry" through the windshield, but I can't stop now. "She doesn't ask because she learned a long time ago that asking doesn't get her anywhere. She just figures it out herself. The bus, the studying, the food, she handles all of it alone because nobody in her life has ever shown up for her."

"That's not—I show up. I told her to come to Pittsburgh. I gave her a place to—"

"A couch, Jason. You gave her a couch, and she was expecting a room. You're a multi-millionaire."

We're at a red light. The arena is three blocks away. I can see the lights from here, the crowd filtering in, the scalpers working the corner. My pulse pounds in my neck, and I know I need to stop talking, but the dam is broken.

"Your sister is the most capable person I've ever met. She does an exceptionally difficult job. And she thinks she's stupid because she has test anxiety when really she just doesn't even have the right materials. And she thinks she's the black sheep of the family, Rookie. It sucks."

The light turns green. I drive. The arena parking garage swallows us, and I pull into our spot and kill the engine. Neither of us moves.

Jason is quiet for a long time. Then he says, very carefully, "Why do you care so much about my sister?"

There it is. The question I can't answer honestly. The honest answer would detonate everything: the friendship, the team, the living situation, the taste of Ella's mouth that I can still feel on my lips and tongue. God, the feel of her body against mine.

"Because I live with her too," I manage. "Because someone has to notice, and you're not."

He flinches. I see it—the micro-movement, the jaw, the way his eyes drop to his hands in his lap. I landed a hit, and we both know it.

He nods once, stiffly, and gets out of the car. I get out, too. We walk into the arena without speaking, through the tunnel, past security, into the locker room where the rest of the team is already suiting up.

The vibe follows us like rink stink. Spinner looks up from taping his stick, and his eyes bounce between us. He opens his mouth and, for once, closes it. Mayhem is already dressed, sitting on the bench, and he watches us walk in quietly, but I can fucking tell that he feels the tension.

I go to my stall. Rookie goes to his. Three stalls apart, and it might as well be a canyon.

I'm pulling on my base layer when I feel a presence beside me. Mayhem, fully padded, smelling like athletic tape and Icy Hot.

"Whatever that is," he says, low enough that only I can hear, "put it in a box. You've got two and a half hours to hold it together."

"I'm good."

"You're not. But you will be." He taps my shin pad with his stick and walks away.

I gear up. Tape my stick. Lace my skates. Go through the motions that have been the same since I was six years old, and try to put the argument in the box like Mayhem said.

Across the room, Rookie is doing the same thing. His jaw is still tight. He hasn't looked at me.

Then Grentley, of all people, the man with the emotional range of a parking meter, walks between our stalls and says, "If you two are going to have a lovers' quarrel, do it after we win." He doesn't stop. He doesn't look back. But the sheer audacity of Josh Grentley making a joke breaks something loose.

A few guys laugh. Spinner cackles. Rookie's mouth twitches. I catch his eye, and something lifts.

I hold out my fist. He looks at it for a beat. Two beats. Then he bumps it, hard enough that I feel it through my glove.

"We're talking about this later," he says.

"Yeah. No shit."

We're not fine. But we can play.

Coach calls us in. We huddle. We break. We hit the tunnel, and the noise of eighteen thousand people fills the concrete corridor, and I let it drown out everything except the burn to destroy Philly and their smug mascot.

But underneath the adrenaline and the anthem and the roar of the crowd, Jason's question sits in my chest like a bruise that hasn't finished forming.

Why do I care so much about his sister?

Why have I spent every moment since the sex lesson replaying the feel of her body under my hand, against my chest, beneath me? All those glorious curves pressed against me, quivering. She said she'd never been touched, yet she knew how to unravel me. She had me begging for more, and she didn't even realize it.

Ella Rujkowski, with her insistence on using my first name, is becoming a major distraction. If I'm not careful, this could mess up my game and my relationship with my best friend.

My phone buzzes during my dinner break — a granola bar and black coffee in the supply closet, because the cafeteria closed an hour ago and I refuse to eat from the vending machine beneath my brother's smug jerky face.

I almost drop my coffee when I see two texts from Jason.

> You can use my laptop if you need it for studying. Password is BAUER$.

> Sending you sum $$ for a cab or whatever.
> We're heading to DC straight from the arena.
> Back Sunday.

I stare at the screen. Jason Rujkowski, the man who weighs his protein powder and once threatened a college teammate for borrowing his stick tape, just offered me his laptop and left me cab money. Unprompted. Without a lecture about the rules.

Something happened. I don't know what happened, but something did.

I text back a quick

> Thank you.

Three dots appear, disappear, appear again.

Yeah. Good luck studying.

That's it. No explanation. No emotional breakthrough. Just Jason doing something thoughtful for the first time in recent memory and immediately retreating before anyone can make a big deal about it.

I'll take it.

———

I get out of my shift only a half hour late and order a ride share for the first time, feeling like royalty in the back seat of a sedan that smells like pine air freshener instead of dried piss. The driver doesn't try to talk to me. The heater works. I tip him generously and feel only a small pang of guilt.

The apartment is empty. Really empty — I have the place to myself for at least three days. They're in DC, then a stop somewhere else, I think. I haven't memorized their schedule.

I drop my bag, shower, and stand in the living room in my pajamas — flannel pants and an old college T-shirt — and notice something I missed this morning in my pre-dawn rush.

Curtains.

Someone hung curtains over the floor-to-ceiling windows. They're simple, dark gray, blackout material, the kind you'd find at any home store, but they transform the room. The living room is no longer a glass box broadcasting my existence to the riverfront. It's enclosed. Private. Mine, at least for the next few days.

I run my hand along the fabric. Did Bernard do this? Had to be him, right? I glance around, and there's no note. I know my brother *just* turned into a human being, but Bernard has been kind to me for over a week. Rides to and from work.

Leftover food. And apparently hanging curtains in a room so I don't feel watched in my temporary home.

I close the curtains, and the apartment wraps around me cozy as a blanket. I duck into my brother's room and grab his laptop, laughing when I see he has the password written on a piece of tape on the case. Snuggling into the sofa with just the stove light on, I pull up the NCLEX prep website.

I've been using the app on my phone, squinting at tiny text on a cracked screen, and the difference is immediate. The questions are larger. The answer choices are spaced apart. I can actually see all four options without scrolling.

But the real discovery happens by accident. I'm poking around in the settings when I find the accessibility features. Text-to-speech. Screen reader. Audio playback of questions.

I click it. A calm, robotic voice reads the first question aloud: "A patient presents with sudden onset chest pain, diaphoresis, and shortness of breath. Which of the following nursing interventions should be performed first?"

And I know the answer. Immediately. No jumbling, no second-guessing, no transposing words. The voice reads the choices, and I click the right one without hesitation.

I take twenty questions. I get sixteen right.

I take twenty more. Eighteen correct.

My hands shake. Not from anxiety — from something else that feels like the ground shifting under my feet, like discovering a door in a room you thought had no exits.

Suddenly, Bernard's playful voice in the car and on this couch seems less like witchcraft and more like a revelation: when information comes in through my ears instead of my eyes, my brain processes it just fine.

I pass a practice test for the first time since I started studying.

I close the laptop and press my hands over my face and breathe, because I am not going to cry on my brother's couch. But something cracks inside me — something old and heavy and calcified — and for the first time I think: maybe I'm not stupid.

————

My roommates' road trip leaves me feeling like I live alone. I drink coffee with no bra on, sleep in my underwear with the heat cranked high.

And, interestingly, I text Bernard Houser. A lot.

It starts with a practical purpose.

BERNARD

Pop quiz. Name the four chambers.

ME

Are you serious?

BERNARD

Name them.

And I do.

BERNARD

Just warming up. What's the normal ejection fraction?

ME

55 to 70 percent. Are you Googling these?

BERNARD

I have a sports medicine textbook in my hotel room.

ME

Why??

BERNARD

Spinner thinks it's a bible. Don't ruin it for him.

The tone shifts.

BERNARD

How was work?

ME

Long. Dislocated shoulder, three lacerations, a guy who swallowed a quarter on a dare.

BERNARD

A quarter.

ME

He was thirty-four years old.

BERNARD

Did you get it out?

ME

That's not really my department. But I did get to watch the X-ray. It was in his esophagus, very shiny, very stupid.

BERNARD

I once swallowed a piece of a mouth guard during a game and didn't tell anyone for three days.

ME

Bernard.

BERNARD

It came out on its own!

ME

I'm choosing not to respond to that.

It shifts again.

BERNARD

I've been thinking about the next lesson.

And that halts me right the hell in my tracks, nipples hard in the living room, grateful for the curtains.

How could I want anything more than kisses with him again? Those sweet touches and shivers... Except I shouldn't want that at all, and he's just doing me a favor to prepare me for the ultimate goal: my own man. Separate from the world of hockey. And yet...

A pause. Dots appearing, disappearing.

That single word sits on my screen and heats me from the inside. I press the phone against my chest and stare at the curtains, think about Bernard's hands on my collarbone and his mouth on mine, and worry that I don't just want to have sex with "a" man to savor that experience.

I'm worried, I want to have sex with that man. Specifically.

Not good.

Aarthi catches me smiling at my phone during a lull and hip-checks me against the nurses' station.

"Who is he?"

"Nobody."

"Nobody is making you grin like a concussed person in a dark hallway? Spill."

McKenzie materializes — she has a sixth sense for gossip, the way I apparently have one for dropping blood pressure. "Who are we talking about? Is it a man? Please tell me it's a man. I need to live vicariously through someone because my love life is an abandoned parking lot."

I shove my phone deep in my scrub shirt pocket. "It's nobody. It's just a friend."

"A friend," Aarthi repeats, in the same tone she uses when a patient says they only had 'one or two drinks.' "Does this friend have a name?"

"Does this friend have a juicy butt?" McKenzie adds.

"I'm not discussing this."

"She's discussing this," Aarthi says to McKenzie. "Give her thirty seconds."

I last twelve. "He's … someone I know from back home. He lives in Pittsburgh. We've been texting each other."

"Texting what?" McKenzie's eyes are enormous.

"Medical trivia, mostly."

They both stare at me. Aarthi puts her hand on my forehead like she's checking for a fever. "Honey. That's foreplay for you?"

I swat her hand away, but I'm smiling, and they see it, and suddenly the three of us are huddled at the nurses' station giggling like we're at a sleepover instead of a trauma center.

"We should hang out," McKenzie says. "Outside of this fluorescent nightmare. Like actual human women who do things that aren't work."

Aarthi claps her hands. "I saw a flyer for an aerial silks class in Lawrenceville," she offers. "It's like circus stuff, but you hang from fabric and feel powerful. My cousin does it in New York and says it changed her life."

"I'm in," I say, before I can overthink it.

The three of us look at each other, and McKenzie grins. "Send us the details?"

"Yes! I love this."

The rest of the shift moves faster after that. I have friends. I have a plan. I have a thing that's mine, not Jason's, not hockey-adjacent, not something I'm doing in the margins of someone else's schedule. For the first time in my life, I'm choosing an activity because it sounds fun and I want to try it.

I take the cab home and text Bernard about it.

> I'm trying circus school this weekend with my nurse friends.

BERNARD

> Like clowns?

ME

> No. Like silks. You hang from long pieces of fabric and do acrobatic things.

BERNARD

> That sounds terrifying.

ME

> Because hockey is so peaceful

BERNARD

> Touché

―――

I've had three glorious days of solo living, and I'm spoiled. I wear what I want, eat what I want, and study whenever the spirit moves me.

This evening, I set up shop on the couch, lying back with Jason's laptop on my legs. The curtains are closed, the lamp's glow is warm, and I'm comfortable in a way that suggests I'm going to drift off midway through my review of medication side effects.

I don't remember falling asleep.

I do become aware of surfacing slowly, the way I always

do, through layers, heavy and warm. There's a hand on my shoulder. Gentle. A voice, low, close.

"Ella. Hey. We're home."

I open my eyes, and Bernard's face is right there. Close. Soft expression, tired eyes, still in his travel suit with the tie loosened. He crouches beside the couch, one hand on my shoulder, and he smells like airplane and coffee, and underneath it, that body wash.

"Bernard," I murmur, and my hand comes up before my brain engages. I touch his jaw. My thumb traces the stubble, the curve of his chin. "You're back."

He goes perfectly still. His eyes search my face, and something passes through them — something warm and unguarded and raw — and for a moment we are just this: his face in my hand, his hand on my shoulder, the lamp casting us in gold.

"I missed you," I say, still half-asleep, still floating in the space where honesty lives because my defenses haven't booted up yet.

Bernard's breath catches.

Then a voice behind him: "She awake?"

Jason. Standing by the front door with his road bag over his shoulder, watching us.

I snap fully conscious. My hand drops from Bernard's face like I've touched a hot stove. I sit upright, clutching the laptop, blinking in the light.

"I'm up. Sorry. I fell asleep studying." I'm already gathering things: laptop, textbook, blanket. "How was the trip?"

"Two and one," Jason says. He's looking at me, then at Bernard, who has straightened up and taken a measured step back from the couch. "You good?"

"Fine. Just tired." I hug the laptop to my chest like a shield. "Thanks for this, by the way. It really helped."

Jason nods. Something flickers across his face, not suspicion exactly, but awareness. Like he's looking at a play he can't quite read yet. "Yeah. No problem."

"Goodnight," I say to both of them, to neither of them, and walk down the hall to Bernard's bedroom and close the door.

I sit on the edge of the bed in the dark.

I press my palms against my eyes and breathe. I crossed a line big time with the guy who is trying to help me out. I remind myself that the physical stuff with Bernard is a favor, lessons, to prepare me for an actual man I have the option of dating.

I touched his face like he was mine. I said I missed him like it was the truest thing I knew. The guy who is best friends with my brother, who lives with him, and plays on a team that's had enough interpersonal conflict. Would the Fury tolerate an explosion between Jason and Bernard?

I am playing with trouble.

But I'm not sure I want to stop.

CHAPTER 10
HOWIE

I crack one eye open and see Ella perched on a stool at the kitchen counter, headphones half-on, Jason's laptop open in front of her. She's in pajama shorts and an oversized T-shirt, bare legs crossed at the ankle, hair piled in a messy knot on top of her head. She's mouthing along with whatever she's hearing in the headphones, occasionally tapping an answer on the screen.

She's fucking gorgeous.

But I can't be having those thoughts. I stretch on the couch, needing to pull all my performance training to the surface so I can focus on what I said I'd do for her. Sex tutoring is basically like a backhand clinic. We're just working on skills.

The road trip nearly killed me. Not the games — we went two and one, which is fine. Not the travel, not the hotels, not Spinner's snoring through the wall. It was the texting with Ella. Every night in my hotel bed, phone in hand, her name on my screen, my brain supplying images I had no business entertaining.

I had to take care of myself in the shower after the "I want" text. Braced against the tile with the water running too hot, thinking about the taste of her mouth, the feel of her collarbone under my fingers, the sounds she made on this couch. I came so hard I saw spots and then stood there with my forehead against the wall, water drumming my back, knowing I was absolutely fucked.

And then I got home, and she touched my face in her sleep and said, "I missed you," and I nearly detonated in front of her brother.

I watch her tap another answer. She does a small fist pump — got it right. My first thought is "that's my girl," but ... that's a dangerous group of words.

I glance around even though I know Jason is out with his nutritionist today. These food acquisition missions are an all-day affair because sourcing Jason's specific elk and bison quotas apparently requires visiting four different farms way out in the boonies.

Which means we have the apartment to ourselves. All day.

I sit up on the couch, letting the blanket fall, and pad barefoot to the kitchen. Ella doesn't hear me — headphones — so when I slide onto the stool beside her, she startles so hard she nearly knocks the laptop off the counter.

"Jesus, Bernard!"

"Sorry. Morning."

She pulls one earphone out, pressing a hand to her chest. I try not to look at the way her T-shirt stretches across her breasts when she does that. I fail. "How long have you been awake?"

"Just woke up. What are you studying?"

"Pharmacology. Reviewing mechanisms of action of cardiac drugs." She turns the laptop toward me, showing the practice interface with the audio controls. "Look at this — the text-to-speech feature reads the questions out loud, and I actually get them right. I've been passing practice sections all week."

She says this like she's reporting game stats, but I can see brightness underneath, the pride she won't let herself fully feel. This is the woman who told me she was stupid. Who evidently believed it.

"That's amazing, Ella."

She presses her lips together. "It's because of you, partly. The way you quiz me in the car... I realized I learn better through listening."

I should not say what pops into my own dumb brain. Yet I hear the words forming, and I don't bother to stop them.

"Well," I say, "I've been told I give great aural."

Ella stares at me. Her mouth twitches. She bites her lower lip, and I watch the color flood her cheeks, and I think: this is it, she's going to throw the laptop at my head. I deserve it.

Instead, she says, very calmly, "Is that so?"

"I mean. So I've heard."

"From whom?"

"A gentleman never tells."

She's smiling now — really smiling, so big her nose crinkles — and the kitchen is warm, and Jason is gone, and she's sitting beside me in shorts with her bare knee almost touching my thigh, and the word "aural" is hanging between us like a lit fuse.

"So," she says. "That means you should totally blab."

The mouth on this girl. I grin at her. "Ella Rujkowski. What are you implying?"

She shrugs. "That you're the kind of guy who gives out sex lessons..."

My pulse kicks. "I am."

"Well." She bites that lip I tasted last week. "I'd like to start the day off right, if that works for you."

If that works for me. If having Ella Rujkowski in my arms works for me. I exhale through my nose and nod, because words have temporarily left my body.

She closes the laptop and climbs down from the stool,

adjusting her hair. "Could we go into the bedroom? Just ... because there's a door."

I nod and follow her in there, wordless. I duck into the bathroom and brush my teeth. The room smells like her— shampoo, fruity deodorant, laundry detergent. When I emerge, Ella sits on the bed facing me, cross-legged, and the confidence from the kitchen is already wavering. I can see it — the shift in her eyes, the way she touches the hem of her T-shirt. She's nervous. The bravado that got her to say "deflower me" over meatballs is different from the vulnerability of being here, in daylight, about to take clothes off.

"We can stop anytime," I tell her. "Any second. You say the word."

"I know."

"I mean it, Ella. This isn't... there's no momentum that can't be stopped. I've got great brakes."

"Did you just compare yourself to a car?" She laughs. The nervousness eases. This is how we work — the joke opens the door, the real thing walks through it.

"Should I take this off?" she asks, touching her T-shirt.

My throat dries. "If you want to."

"I've never—nobody's seen me. Without a shirt."

"Ella, you don't have to—"

She pulls it over her head.

She's not wearing a bra. She's just there, an adult Ella Rujkowski, bare from the waist up, sitting on my bed in the morning light, and she is the most beautiful thing I have ever seen.

Her breasts are full and heavy, soft, with dark nipples that are already peaked from the cool air or nervousness or desire or all three. Her stomach is round and soft, and there's a scatter of freckles across her chest that I didn't know existed and now constitute my entire reason for living.

She crosses her arms.

I reach forward and gently pull them apart. "Don't."

"I'm—it's a lot. I know I'm—"

"Ella." My voice comes out rougher than I intend. "You are so fucking gorgeous. I need you to hear me. Any man who is ever lucky enough to see you like this better worship the opportunity, or I will personally wring his neck."

The words land between us, and I hear what I just said — the possessiveness, the violence of it. But that's what we're doing here, preparing her for a datable guy.

"Can I touch you?" I ask.

"Yes."

I climb onto the bed beside her and start where I started last time — her jaw, her neck, her collarbone. Known territory. She exhales, and I feel her settle. But this time, when my fingers reach the edge where the fabric stopped me before, there's no fabric. Just skin. Warm, soft, impossibly smooth skin that gives under my fingertips as I trace down from her collarbone to the swell of her breast.

I cup her in my palm, and her breath catches so hard I feel it in my own lungs. She's looking down, watching my hand on her, and her lips are parted, and her eyes are wide, and I realize she's never had anyone's hands here. Not like this. Not with intention and desire and the kind of reverence that makes my own hands shake.

"Okay?" I murmur.

"Don't stop."

I brush my thumb across her nipple. She gasps and grabs my forearm, fingers digging in. The sound she makes is small and sharp and goes straight to my groin like an electric current.

"Bernard—"

"I'm here."

"I want to see you too."

Fair is fair. I pull my T-shirt over my head and drop it on the floor. She stares at my chest with an expression I'd describe as clinical if her pupils weren't blown black.

"I've seen shirtless men," she says, like she's trying to maintain professional distance. "In hockey arenas and a medical context."

"How's this context?"

"Different." Her hand comes up and flattens against my sternum. "Very different."

"Your turn. Touch wherever."

She explores me the way she did before — methodical, curious, thorough. Fingers tracing muscle groups she can name, mapping my scars, testing what makes me react. But bare skin-to-bare skin changes everything. When she drags her nails down my ribs, I shudder. When she traces the line of hair below my navel, I stop breathing.

"Can I see ..." She gestures vaguely downward, and I feel every drop of blood in my body change direction.

"Yeah. If you want."

I stand. Thumbs in the waistband. Hesitate. "Fair warning, I'm not snipped. Some women think it's weird looking."

"I've seen uncircumcised penises, Bernard. I'm a nurse."

"Right. Clinical context. This is—"

"Different. I know." She looks at me steadily, expectant, and I push my sweatpants and boxers down and stand there under Ella Rujkowski's gaze, somehow the most vulnerable I have felt in my entire life, including every locker room and every doctor's office and every time I've been naked in front of another human being.

She looks. Really studies, with the focused attention she gives everything, and her lips part and she says, "Oh."

"Good oh or..."

She swallows. "You're ... proportional."

"Proportional?"

"To the rest of you. Which is very large."

I feel my face split into a grin I couldn't suppress if Coach himself were standing behind me. "Ella Rujkowski, you like my big cock?"

"It was an anatomical observation." But she blushes, and smiles, and looks at me like I'm a specimen she'd very much like to study further, and I'm so hard it actually hurts.

I sit back down beside her, both of us stripped — me fully, her from the waist up — and pull a blanket across my lap because I need to focus, and that's impossible while she's sneaking glances at my dick.

"Today's about you," I tell her. "I want to make you feel good so you know what you like. Can I?"

"Yes."

I lay her back and settle next to her, leaning over her but not giving her my full weight because she's right. I'm big as fuck. I kiss her, slow at first, the way I now know she likes, then deeper when she pulls at me. I kiss her jaw, her neck, the hollow of her throat where her pulse hammers.

I kiss her collarbone, and she sighs. I kiss lower. She holds her breath. I close my mouth over her nipple, and she arches off the mattress with a sound that rewires my brain entirely.

I take my time. There is nothing in the world more important than this — the way she responds, the sounds I'm learning, the map of her body I'm drawing with my mouth. She's responsive in a way that tells me everything about the kind of lover she'll be: present, unguarded, honest in her body even when she's guarded everywhere else.

Her boobs are my fantasy of what perfect boobs should look and feel like. Everything about them lights me up inside. But I'm supposed to be showing her what feels good.

My hand slides down her stomach, over the soft curve of her belly, to the waistband of her shorts. I pause with my hand on a set of silvery stretch marks that match the ones on my own hips where I bulked up long ago. "Okay?"

"Please."

"So, basically, this is like the bare minimum you should expect from a guy you're with." The thought of another man doing this with her tenses all the muscles in my neck. But I'm teaching here. "You need to be hearing how perfect you look. How incredible your body feels."

"It does?" Her eyes are so big and confused, like she somehow doesn't know what she looks like.

I swallow. "It really does." I slip my hand beneath the fabric. When I touch her mound, she makes a sound I will remember for the rest of my life — half gasp, half moan, a crack in everything she holds together — and her hand flies to my wrist. Not to stop me. To hold me there.

"Tell me what feels good," I murmur against her neck.

"That. That feels..." she pauses, swallowing a breath, "Bernard, oh my god."

I keep my finger where she wants it, circling slowly. I find the right pressure, the right place, guided by the grip of her hand on my wrist and the pitch of her breathing and the way her hips move in these small, desperate circles that are absolutely wrecking me.

She has no idea how hot it is that she's guiding me instinctively, asking so clearly for what she wants and needs. I'm hard against her thigh, and I ignore it completely because this is about her, only her, and I want this to be so good she never forgets it.

"I'm...something's..." Her voice is tight, climbing, eyes wide and glistening, so bright.

"Let it happen, Ella. I've got you."

She comes with her face pressed against my shoulder and her hand clenched around my wrist. I don't even have a finger inside her, just pressed against her clit, but I feel her body pulsing, contracting. I hold her through it, solid, steady, whispering her name.

She's quiet for a long time after. Breathing. Eyes closed. Her hand loosens on my wrist, but doesn't let go. I don't move. I barely breathe. I let her slide back to herself in her own time.

"That was—" She opens her eyes. They're glassy. "Was that—"

"That was a super-hot orgasm," I say, because she deserves to name it.

"From someone else."

I blink, needing not to imagine her getting herself off alone, in my bed, without me.

"Bernard. That was ..." She shakes her head. "Different."

"Good different?"

"I don't have a vocab word for what that was."

I press my forehead against her temple and breathe her in and try very, very hard not to think about what I want, which is to be inside her, which is never to let anyone else touch her, which is to burn the "right guy" framework to the ground and tell her there is no other guy, there's only me, there's only this.

I can't resist bringing my hand to my mouth and licking the taste of her from my fingers. My new favorite flavor.

"What about you?" she asks, shifting against me, obviously feeling the situation at my hip.

"I'm good."

"Bernard, you're clearly—"

"Ella." I pull back and look at her. "That was a complete experience. You don't owe me anything."

She studies me with those sharp nurse eyes. "You're sure?"

"I'm sure."

"Okay," she has a hand on my arm. "But I do need to learn how to..." Ella gestures lewdly, and a strangled sound flies out of my throat.

I scoot back on the bed. "Don't you have circus school?"

She laughs, still dazed, still flushed, and I help her sit up, handing her T-shirt back, watching her pull it on and smooth her hair, all composure and deflection settling back over her like armor. She stands, wobbles slightly, and steadies herself on the arm of the couch.

"Aerial silks," she corrects.

"Sure."

She looks at me for a beat. Something moves behind her eyes, not quite gratitude, not quite affection, something deeper and more dangerous. "Thank you, Bernard."

She disappears into the en suite. The shower starts. I hear her through the wall, moving around in the bathroom, and I sit on my bed with a throw blanket on my lap and her taste on my lips and the phantom grip of her hand around my wrist, and I try to breathe.

She emerges fifteen minutes later in leggings and a tank top, hair wet. She smiles and rummages in her suitcase, still packed with stacks of folded clothes. She stands with a tote bag and grabs her water bottle from my dresser. "I'm meeting Aarthi and McKenzie outside. I'll be back by…"

"I'll pick you up. Text me the address."

She hesitates, then nods. "Okay."

The door closes behind her.

I sit in the silence.

The apartment echoes with sex smells and the ghost of the sound she made when she came. I am so hard I could pound nails, and so emotionally compromised I might need to call the team doctor.

I go to the bathroom. Turn on the shower she just vacated. Step in under water that's too hot and brace one hand against the tile, a position that's becoming routine for me, the longer I live with Rookie's sister. The position of a man who is losing control. I start to move my fist along my length.

I close my eyes and see her face. Relaxed. Open. Beautiful. The way she looked in the moment after, when every wall she had built was down, and she was just Ella, undone, in my arms.

I come fast and hard and stand there with the water hitting my back, breathing.

She's training for the right guy. Not me. I keep saying it.

Preparing her for the right guy. Some future man who'll get to touch her, hold her, and make her make that sound.

The thought makes me want to put my fist through the tile.

I can't be the right guy. She's my best friend's sister. She's living in my apartment because she has nowhere else to go.

But the idea of another man's hands where mine just were — another man learning the sounds she makes, the way she arches, the grip of her fingers — fills me with a rage so white-hot it scares me.

I turn off the water. Dry off. Get dressed.

I sit on the couch where she lay twenty minutes ago, and I text Mayhem.

> You free?

MAYHEM

What's up?

ME

Nothing. Can we get meatballs?

MAYHEM

I'll be there in 20.

I put my phone down and press my palms against my eyes.

This was supposed to be a favor.

I am so far past favors I can't even see them in the rearview.

CHAPTER 11
ELLA

AARTHI PICKS ME UP IN A DENTED HONDA CIVIC WITH A READY TO WED bumper sticker her mother put on before Aarthi could stop her. McKenzie is already in the back seat with two iced coffees and a bag of cashews.

"Fuel," she says, thrusting a coffee at me. "We're going to need upper body strength, and I have been surviving on vending machine Doritos."

The aerial silks studio is in a converted warehouse in Lawrenceville, on a block that also has a ramen shop and a tattoo parlor. Inside, it smells like chalk and rubber mats, and long panels of purple and red fabric hang from the ceiling like something out of Peter Pan. I count eight silks, each pooling on the floor in graceful heaps, and a handful of women already stretching on mats.

We find a spot near the back and spread out. McKenzie touches her toes with ease. Aarthi sits cross-legged and pulls one arm across her chest, grimacing. I bend forward and feel the burn of a twelve-hour shift in every muscle south of my ribcage.

"So," McKenzie says, switching arms. "Aarthi, we need to discuss that bumper sticker."

Aarthi groans. "My mother sent me seven — seven —

profiles on a matrimonial site this week. One of the men listed his hobby as 'breathing.' Another one's photo was clearly taken at a funeral."

"A funeral?"

"He was standing next to a casket, McKenzie. In a suit. Smiling."

"Maybe he was happy to be there." McKenzie bites a pretzel. "My update is that I got a DM from Kyle."

"Kyle the ex?" I ask.

"The shit burger. He said, and I quote, 'I've considered what you said and think you should return to Kentucky for some growth work.'" She gags. "Growth work. He can't even grow a full beard."

"So that's a no," Aarthi says.

"That is a block, delete, and sage my phone." McKenzie pulls a leg practically behind her ear, demonstrating incredible flexibility I'm not envious of at all. "What I actually want is to just … get laid. No feelings. No growth work. Just a nice man with a functional body and low expectations." She turns to me. "Ella. Your brother is a professional hockey player."

"Unfortunately."

"Doesn't he have friends? Aren't hockey guys like, famously …" She waves a foot in the air. "Available?"

Aarthi snorts. "She means slutty."

"I mean open to casual encounters with consenting women."

I open my mouth to respond — to say something about the parade of women I've witnessed filtering through my brother's rooms over the years — but the instructor claps her hands and saves me from a conversation I am absolutely not ready to navigate, given that I had a hockey player's hand down my shorts a few hours ago.

The teacher's voice booms, as if she has practiced broadcasting to a full room. "Welcome, everyone! I'm Jules. Let's start with some basics."

Jules appears white, maybe five foot two, and built like a gymnast, with arms that suggest she could bench-press most of the women in this room. She radiates the calm authority I associate with charge nurses, no nonsense, but Jules is also kind.

We start on the ground. I listen as she explains grip technique: wrap the silk around your hands, pull it taut, feel the tension in your shoulders. My forearms burn almost immediately. Pumping up pressure bags and restraining combative patients in the ER have given me functional strength, but this is different. This requires me to hold my own body weight, which is not insignificant, and trust that a piece of fabric won't let me go.

"Grip higher," Jules tells me, adjusting my hands. "Good. Now pull yourself up. Use your core, not just your arms."

I pull. My feet leave the ground by about two inches, and I immediately drop back down.

"That's perfect for your first time," Jules says. "Try again."

It feels humiliating, far from perfect. McKenzie, who apparently has hidden lizard DNA, scrambles up her silk with ease. Aarthi manages a wobbly hang. I try again and get slightly higher, arms shaking, the fabric biting into my palms.

"Use the foot lock," Jules says, crouching beside me. "Step on the silk with your right foot. Wrap it around your arch. Now the fabric carries some of your weight."

I do as she says, and something clicks. The silk catches under my arch, and suddenly I'm not fighting gravity alone. The fabric holds me, supports me. I pull up, wrap my foot tighter, and I'm suspended, a fairy. Flying. Three feet off the ground, gripping the silk above me, one leg wrapped and locked, the other extended into open air.

It's not graceful. My arms shake. My face is probably purple. But I'm up. I'm off the ground. My body — this body that I've spent years thinking of as too big, too much, taking up too much space in too many backseats — holds me in the air.

"Beautiful!" Jules claps. "Hold it. Breathe."

I breathe, thinking of Bernard offering the same suggestion and feeling my body flush all over. I look down at my hands wrapped in purple silk, my knuckles white, my forearms straining. My leg extends in the air, pointed in a way I choose to imagine is graceful. My core is engaged, working, and strong.

I tilt my head back and laugh. I can't help it. The sound erupts from somewhere deep and joyful, and it bounces off the warehouse ceiling, and McKenzie whoops from her silk, and Aarthi cheers from the mat where she's given up and sprawled on her back.

I feel incredible. I feel powerful. I feel like my body is a machine. I've been doubting my entire life, and someone just proved it works.

I arch my neck in triumph, chin up, grinning at the ceiling — and through the studio's front window, half-obscured by the logo stenciled on the glass, I see a face.

Bernard.

He stands on the sidewalk with his hands in his jacket pockets, watching me. His expression is strange. Not smiling, not frowning. He looks caught between wonder and ache, like he's squinting at something bright he knows he shouldn't stare at.

My stomach flips. I wobble on the silk, tightening my grip.

He came early to pick me up, and now I'm on display like the prow of a ship, but he sure doesn't seem horrified. His face looks a little like it did when I first took my shirt off for my first lesson of the day. But I can't think about that now, while I'm in a different lesson entirely.

Jules calls time. I lower myself, less gracefully than I'd like, more controlled than I expected, and land on the mat.

My arms are jelly. My palms are raw and pink. I feel like I could run through a wall.

"That was INCREDIBLE," McKenzie announces, dropping from her silk and grabbing my arm. "Ella, you're a natural."

"I was up for like twelve seconds."

"You looked like a glorious bird. We're coming back next week."

Aarthi joins us, rolling her shoulders in agony. "My cousin is a liar. That was not empowering. That was assault by fabric." She flexes her reddened hands. "But I'll come back because you two clearly need supervision."

We gather our things and head for the door. I'm pulling on my hoodie when McKenzie spots Bernard through the window. He leans against the G-Wagon, scrolling his phone, looking every inch the professional athlete at rest: expensive jacket, expensive car, effortless posture.

"Is *that* your ride?" McKenzie's voice pitches up half an octave.

"That's my roommate. He offered to pick me up."

"Your roommate. A hockey player." McKenzie grabs my arm. "Ella. You failed to mention that your roommate looks like that."

"He's my brother's friend."

"He's a threat to panties everywhere." She's already pushing through the studio door. "We should get drinks. All of us. Does he have more friends? Friends who want to have a casual drink with three sweaty nurses in tight pants?"

I don't have a chance to answer because we're on the sidewalk now, and Bernard looks up from his phone, and his face transforms when he sees me — a flash, quick, the private look from the window — before it folds into something else entirely.

I watch the volume on his personality turn up until he's nothing like the tender Bernard from earlier today.

"Ladies," he says, pocketing his phone and standing tall. His voice is louder, warmer, pitched for an audience. This isn't the man who whispered my name against my neck. This is Howie Houser, professional charmer, the guy who knows every bouncer in Pittsburgh. "How was clown college?"

"Aerial silks," I correct, trying to control this situation and failing.

"It was amazing," McKenzie says, extending her hand. "I'm McKenzie. Ella's friend from work. We're nurses."

"Howie." He shakes her hand with both of his, and I watch McKenzie lick her lips. "I've heard great things. You're the one from Louisville, right?"

She melts. Actually melts on the frigid sidewalk. He deployed that factoid like a heat-seeking missile of personal charm.

"And you must be Aarthi." He turns to her with the same warmth, the same focus.

Aarthi, who is immune to most forms of nonsense, cracks a reluctant smile. "She talks about us?"

"Constantly." He glances at me, and our eyes catch for half a second, long enough for me to see the real Bernard underneath the Howie show — before he snaps back to performing. "So what's the plan? You guys hungry? Thirsty?"

"We want drinks," McKenzie says. "And Ella says hockey players are fun."

"I absolutely did not say that."

"You implied it." McKenzie turns to Bernard with the confidence of a woman who has fully decided to shoot her shot. "Do you have single friends who might want to meet three incredibly interesting women who just defied gravity?"

Bernard laughs. The big, public one, the Howie laugh, the one that carries half a block, and pulls out his phone. "I might know a guy or two. Where do you want to go?"

McKenzie names a bar nearby. Aarthi suggests a backup.

Bernard's thumbs fly across his screen, and I stand on the sidewalk watching him text his teammates, watching my careful, private world tilt on its axis toward my brother's loud, public one.

This is Howie. The party organizer. The social connector. The man half of Pittsburgh has seen buying rounds for strangers. And I'm standing here in a sweaty tank top with chalk dust on my hands and silk burn on my palms, watching him charm the two people who see me as just Ella — not Baby Rookie, not a hockey player's sister, just Ella. I feel the ground shift.

For the last ten days, I've had Bernard. Private, tender, devastating Bernard, who quizzes me on cardiac conduction and traces my collarbone and tells me I'm gorgeous with a voice like gravel. I've had him in a bubble — the apartment, the car, his bed.

Now my friends are meeting Howie. And Howie is spectacular— magnetic, generous, impossible not to like. But he's not the man who held me while I shook apart this morning. He's the version of that man built for public consumption, and I'm the only person on this sidewalk who knows the difference.

Bernard catches my eye again over McKenzie's head. One look. Quick. The grin stays on his face, but something behind his eyes flickers — a question, a check-in, the real him surfacing for just a breath.

You okay?

I give him the smallest nod.

He goes back to making my friends laugh. McKenzie asks about the G-Wagon. Aarthi pretends she's not impressed but keeps glancing at the car. Bernard tells a story about Spinner that has both of them cackling, and I watch him work — this gift he has, this ability to make everyone feel included, seen, important — and I think about how nobody sees him.

They see Howie. The party. The fun.

They don't see Bernard, who woke up early to drive a woman to work because nobody else thought to. Who hung curtains without being asked. Who held my wrist while I came and then told me I didn't owe him a thing.

CHAPTER 12
HOWIE

THE BAR MCKENZIE PICKED HAS EXPOSED BRICK, STRING LIGHTS, and a cocktail menu that Spinner studies like game tape. Mayhem takes up way more than his fair share of space in the booth and nurses a single beer, watching the room with a menacing stare.

I thought I could just confess my sins to him over meatballs earlier today, but in the end, I chickened out and just said it's overwhelming sharing a two-bedroom apartment with three people. Except that motherfucker read between the lines. I know it.

Ella sits across from me between her friends. She is killing me with that body of hers displayed in tights, and her cheeks are still flushed from the exercise. Every time she laughs at something McKenzie says, I feel it in my sternum like a body check.

I can't stop seeing her in the silk. The arch of her back. The line of her extended leg was thick and round in all the right places. The way she tipped her chin up and laughed and looked like something out of a painting, powerful and suspended, held by her own strength.

I want to put my mouth on the inside of her wrist. I want

to trace the silk marks on her palms with my tongue. I want to…

"Howie." Spinner snaps his fingers in my face. "You in there?"

"Yeah. What?"

"I asked if you want another round." He gestures at the table, which has accumulated a modest graveyard of glasses. "McKenzie's buying."

"I absolutely am not," McKenzie says. "I'm a nurse with college loans. I make less than your dry cleaner."

"Then I'm buying." Spinner stands, grinning, and McKenzie gives him a look that suggests Louisville may be permanently in her rearview. "What does everyone want?"

He takes orders. McKenzie follows him to the bar to "help carry," which fools nobody. Aarthi excuses herself for the restroom.

For approximately eleven seconds, it's just me, Ella, and Mayhem.

Ella takes a sip of her drink and looks at me over the rim. Her eyes say everything her mouth can't in this room full of people. I look back and try to keep my face in Howie mode, but I can feel it slipping, the mask getting thin, because earlier today this woman came apart under my hand and now she's sitting across from me in a crowded bar pretending we're just roommates.

"You guys are cute," Mayhem says, not looking up from his beer.

Ella's glass freezes halfway to her mouth. I feel my spine go rigid. "What?"

He waves a hand toward Ella. "You and the group." He takes a slow sip. "Nice that you're making friends."

I stare at him. His face reveals nothing. Mayhem is either the most oblivious man alive or the most perceptive, and I have never once been able to tell the difference.

"Yeah," I manage. "It's good."

He nods. Sips. Stares at the table. Then, so quiet I almost miss it: "Be careful."

Before I can respond, Spinner returns with drinks and McKenzie on his arm, and the moment dissolves into noise and laughter and the safety of a group. Aarthi comes back and starts grilling Mayhem about what he's reading. Spinner tells a story about a road trip in juniors, that has McKenzie wheezing.

Ella laughs, and her knee bumps mine under the table and stays there, warm through my denim, and I leave it. I leave it right there and drink my beer and perform Howie Houser, life of the party, man with nothing to hide.

McKenzie asks Ella something about work, and Ella launches into a story about a patient whose roommate put glue in the toothpaste tube, and I watch her friends lean in, rapt, laughing, and I realize: she's funny. Not just dry-humor funny with me, but commanding-a-table funny. Her timing is perfect. She does voices. McKenzie throws a napkin at her, and Aarthi wipes her eyes. Ella glows with it, the pleasure of being seen as entertaining and interesting and wanted for something other than her proximity to a hockey player.

I could watch her all night. That's the problem.

Mayhem nudges my boot under the table. I tear my eyes away from Ella, and he gives me a look that says, louder than words: I said be careful.

—————

The energy level at morning practice is what I'd expect from the Fury in pre-season. We shouldn't have gone out on a weeknight. Spinner skates onto the ice, singing something off-key. Rookie grumbles about being left out — nobody invited him to the bar, but he was out hunting elk burgers anyway.

"You guys went to a bar without me?" Jason tapes his stick at the bench, looking wounded. "With my sister?"

"We ran into her," Spinner says, which is technically true in the sense that everything is technically something. "She was out with nurse friends. We got drinks. It was chill."

"Who's we?"

"Me, Howie, Mayhem. And Ella's friends." Spinner grins in a way that suggests McKenzie's phone number is saved in his contacts. "One of them is from Kentucky. She does this thing with her…"

"Don't want to hear it," Rookie says.

Coach blows the whistle, and we line up for drills. I feel decent, a little loose from the beer, a little tight from sleeping on the couch, but my legs are under me, and my head is clear. Clearer than it's been in weeks, actually, which is ironic given that my life is a ticking bomb of secrets and desire.

We scrimmage. First unit against second unit, full contact, coaches watching from the bench. I'm on the second line with Spinner, running a cycle play along the boards. The puck dumps into the corner, and I chase it, shoulder down, cutting hard to beat the defenseman to the wall.

What happens next takes about two seconds.

The defender, a rookie named Hargrove who outweighs me by twenty pounds, catches my outside knee with his hip as I cut left. It's not dirty. It's not even hard, really. It's just the wrong angle at the wrong speed, my blade catching a rut in the ice at the exact moment his weight hits my leg.

The pain is instant and specific — a hot, bright flare on the inside of my knee, the kind that makes your vision go white at the edges. I go down. Not dramatically, not with a scream. I just fold, one leg buckling, and hit the ice on my side with my stick clattering away.

The whistle blows. Hargrove skids to a stop and says, "Shit, Howie, I'm sorry—" and I wave him off because it's not his fault, and I can already tell this is bad.

Not catastrophic. I've had catastrophic shoulder surgery and a broken orbital bone. This isn't that. But when I try to put weight on it, the knee says no in a very clear voice. The trainer is already jogging across the ice with that look they get when they're calculating weeks instead of days.

"Don't move," he says. "Let me see."

He bends my knee. Presses on the inside. I grab the boards and squeeze until my knuckles crack.

"MCL," he says. "Almost certainly. We'll get imaging, but I can feel the laxity."

I'm not cramming for an anatomy exam like Ella, but I know that word is no good.

"How long?" I ask.

"Depends on the grade. Could be a week. Could be four."

I lie back on the ice and stare at the ceiling — the lights, the banners, the rafters — and feel the cold seep through my jersey into my back. The team has three road games this week. A swing through Carolina and Florida.

Spinner appears above me, upside down from my vantage point. "You good?"

"MCL."

"Fuck." He taps my chest with his glove. "That sucks, bruh."

Mayhem skates up behind Spinner, silent, looming. He looks down at me, and I look up at him, and he says nothing, because Mayhem never says what he doesn't need to. But I see something flicker across his face — not just concern about my knee. Something else. Something that says: you're about to be alone in that apartment with her for a week.

I know, I want to tell him. *I know.*

Rookie skates over last. "Howie. Shit. You okay?"

"I'll live."

"You need anything? Want me to call Benny?" It's cute that Rookie thinks my agent would respond to this.

"Nah. I'll deal with it." I let the trainer and Spinner help me up, wobbling on one leg, gripping their shoulders. The knee throbs with every heartbeat, hot and swollen already, and I can feel it stiffening as the adrenaline wears off.

Tucker and Alder Stag skate up behind Spinner, the three of them insisting someone call my agent while I'm getting checked out. I hear them joking about how *their* agent probably already knows I'm hurt, and I wonder again if this Benny guy my dad found was another terrible decision in my long list.

The guys get me to the training room and half out of my gear so the trainer can strap a bag of ice to my knee. They have me on my back, my leg elevated, when Coach comes by. He squeezes my shoulder with a "tough luck, kid," and then I hear the staff read my sentence to him: two weeks, no practice, no games.

I watch the rest of practice through the glass. Rookie and Spinner run drills. Mayhem lays someone out with a clean check that echoes across the empty arena. Grentley makes a save I have to admit is beautiful. The Stag brothers whoop and cheer like they don't hate Grentley's guts, and maybe they're slowly getting over their feud.

All I know is they're going to take that energy to Carolina tomorrow morning, and I won't be on that plane.

Micky the trainer insists on a home visit, following me into Rookie's condo, frowning as I install myself on the couch. He sets me up with a foam wedge for elevation and texts me rehab instructions I probably won't read. "I'll see myself out," he says. "And then we'll see you for PT in the morning, okay?"

I grunt, and then the apartment is empty. Ella's at work. Jason's not home from practice and film.

I lie on the couch with my knee throbbing and my head spinning, and I stare at the ceiling where the streetlights used to paint yellow streaks before I hung curtains for a woman I'm not supposed to care about.

And now Ella and I will be alone in this apartment for at least five days, and I can't run, can't skate, can't even walk to Gianna's without limping.

I'm grounded. Trapped. Alone with her.

I press the ice pack harder against my knee and close my eyes.

SUSAN TURNS THE VOLUME UP ON THE WAITING ROOM TV, AND I hear Bernard's name before I see his face.

"—Houser listed as week-to-week with a lower body injury. The Fury forward went down during practice yesterday and did not travel with the team for their three-game road swing through Carolina and Florida—"

I grab the edge of the nurses' station. The screen shows Bernard in his jersey, skating, whole and healthy, with a red graphic that says INJURED stamped across the bottom.

"Isn't that your brother's teammate?" Susan nods at the TV. "MCL, sounds like. I should look him up in the system to see if he's having surgery here."

I ignore Susan's faux-privacy-violation threats and pull out my phone to text Bernard.

> Are you okay?? I just saw the news.

Nothing. No dots. No response.
I text Jason.

> What happened to Bernard?

Three minutes later, my brother says,

I stare at the word "fine" and want to throw my phone at the vending machine with my brother's face on it. "Fine" is the word Jason uses for everything — fine when he offered me a couch, fine when he didn't pick me up from the airport, fine when his best friend apparently hurt a ligament and is lying alone in their apartment.

The rest of my shift is a blur. I cycle between patients and my phone, checking for a response from Bernard that never comes. My brain fills the silence with clinical information I didn't know I'd retained: MCL sprains are graded 1 through 3. Grade 1 is mild, microscopic tears, one to three weeks. Grade 2 is a partial tear, four to six weeks. Grade 3 is a full rupture and surgery. Treatment includes ice, compression, elevation. Limited weight-bearing. No lateral movement.

I know the anatomy. I know the rehab protocol. I know what an MCL does — because I've been studying it on a laptop and in a car with a man who turns medical terminology into foreplay.

What I don't know is how bad it is, whether he's in pain, whether anyone is with him, or whether he's eaten.

I clock out at seven-thirty, skip the bus, and spend Jason's remaining money on a ride share that gets me home in twelve minutes.

The apartment is dim. Jason's door is open, and his room is stripped: road bag gone, open closet half-empty. He's long gone. The living room is quiet except for the TV on low volume, playing something Bernard clearly isn't watching.

He's on the couch. Not casually lounging. Genuinely immobilized. His right knee is wrapped in a compression sleeve and propped on a foam wedge, with a melted ice pack draped across it, doing absolutely nothing therapeutic. He's in mesh shorts and a Fury T-shirt that's wrinkled like he slept in it. His curls are matted on one side. He looks exhausted, bored, and a little defeated.

"Hey," he says, looking up when I come in.

"You didn't text me back."

"My phone died. Charger's in the kitchen and I can't—" He gestures at his knee.

I grab his charger from the counter, plug in his phone, and set it on the ottoman beside a glass of water that looks like it's been sitting there for hours. Then I crouch beside the couch and start unwrapping his knee.

"Ella, what the—"

"This ice pack is room temperature. When did you last swap it?"

"I don't know. Trainer set me up after PT and then—"

"Hours ago?" I peel back the compression sleeve and examine his knee. Swollen, warm to the touch, bruised along the medial side. I palpate gently, and he hisses. "Sorry. Can you bend it?"

"Some." He mumbles something about NSAIDs and grade one sprains while I poke around his knee.

I rewrap it properly, snug but not tight, the way I'd do it for a patient. I go to the freezer and grab a fresh gel pack, slide it carefully inside the wrap, and press it against the swollen joint. My hands know what they're doing. This is my language: injury, care, competence.

Bernard watches me work as if nobody has ever fussed over him like this.

I look at this enormous man on the couch — rumpled, grateful, soft-eyed, watching me with his busted knee elevated. His curls are a disaster. A thought arrives fully formed: St. Bernard. The rescue dog. Huge, gentle, bred to find people lost in the snow and carry them somewhere warm. He's been doing search and rescue on me since the airport, hauling me out of snowdrifts I didn't even know I was buried in.

His voice croaks as he says, "My dad is irate. Says I'm throwing away my career by *skipping* ice time."

I hum a response. The Housers have always been hard on him. Even Jason, who has the emotional intelligence of a helmet, has mentioned that a few times through the years. Bernard's dad played in the pros, too, but his career was cut short after some sort of scandal. Bernard doesn't talk about it.

"Have you eaten?" I ask.

"I had a protein bar a while ago."

"Bernard, you are a finely tuned machine. You need fuel."

"I can't really get to the kitchen."

I stand and smirk. "Want me to heat up some bison balls for us to share?"

He guffaws. "I don't know if that sounds appetizing, but there's takeout from Gianna's if you don't mind getting that for me?"

I pop the food in the oven and rush through a shower before bringing my patient a bowl with a fork and a fresh glass of water. He eats sitting up, his leg still elevated, and I perch on the edge of the ottoman, facing him, because all the chairs are too far away and I want to be close.

"Thank you," he says between bites. "You didn't have to do all this."

"You drove me to work every day for two weeks. I think I can manage an ice pack."

He smiles. Eats another meatball. Then, with the careful tone of a man navigating a field of landmines: "So. Jason's gone."

"I noticed."

"For at least five days."

"I'm aware."

He sets the bowl down. "Ella, I've been thinking."

"Dangerous."

"About the whole … tutoring situation." He rubs the back of his neck. "The plan was to prepare you for the right guy, and I just realized, you were out at a bar with us the other night. With Spinner and Mayhem and a room full of available men. And you didn't … you know. Try to meet anyone."

I stare at him. "You're asking why I didn't pick up a man at the bar?"

"I'm asking why you didn't take the opportunity to—"

"To what? Flirt with someone in front of my brother's teammates?" I lean back. "Bernard, that's literally why I'm a forty-year-old virgin." He opens his mouth to argue about my age, but I hold up a palm. "Every guy I ever talk to gets scared off by Jason or his teammates. I can't go looking for a man in the same circles where my brother has already posted a 'don't touch my sister' sign."

He opens his mouth again, but closes it this time. I can see him processing, the closed loop of my brother's world, the way it shrinks my options to zero.

"So what's your plan to meet your man?" he asks.

"When? Between my twelve-hour shifts and my studying? When exactly am I meeting this mythical right guy?"

Bernard snorts. "Not at clown college, that's for sure." He shifts on the couch, wincing as his knee protests while his words sting me. "I still don't get why you didn't just try a normal sport."

The words land differently than he intends them. I can tell by the casual way he says it — the same way Jason would say it, the same way my dad would say it. Like it's a joke.

"When would I have learned a sport, Bernard?"

His face changes.

"My entire childhood was hockey. *Jason's* hockey. His practices, his games, his tournaments, his showcases. Every weekend. Every summer. Every family vacation was actually a hockey camp disguised as a trip." I keep my voice level because this isn't anger, it's just fact. "I did my homework in the back of the car. I ate dinner in arena parking lots. My dad spent every spare dollar on ice time, private coaching, and travel fees, and my mom spent every spare hour driving us to his development activities. There wasn't time for me to do a sport. There wasn't money for me to do a sport. I was an accessory."

Bernard stares at me. I watch the realization move across his face like fog off the Allegheny River. He was IN that car. He was one of the hockey boys who took up the space. He just never looked at it from my side of the backseat.

"The silks are the first hobby I have ever chosen for myself," I say. "The first activity I have done because I wanted to, not because someone else's schedule required me to be somewhere adjacent to it. So no, I didn't try a *normal* sport. I was too busy being a passenger in someone else's life."

He's quiet for a long time. His jaw works. I can see him re-processing — every childhood memory, every carpool, every tournament where I sat in the stands with a textbook while he and Jason played the game that mattered.

"I'm sorry," he says.

"Don't worry about it."

The silence between us is heavy but not hostile. It's the stillness of something settling into place, a joint clicking back into alignment.

I look at his knee. My hand is still resting on the ice pack, holding it against the joint. My fingers curve over the edge of the wrap, touching the bare skin of his thigh beneath the hem of his shorts.

I don't move my hand. Neither does he.

"So anyway, I still need to learn the arts of love," I say.

His eyes drop to my hand on his leg. "Ella..."

I slide my hand an inch higher on his thigh. His quad tenses under my palm. "If you're not in pain, this seems like a good time for extra credit." The leg muscles quiver beneath my hand. I hold his gaze. "Teach me how to make you feel good, Bernard."

His throat moves. I watch him swallow, watch his hands grip the couch cushion, watch the war play out across his features — the part of him that wants to keep giving and never receive versus the part of him that's been turning this down since our first lesson.

"You don't have to…"

"I know I don't have to. I want to." I move my hand higher. His breath stutters. "You've been taking care of me since I got to Pittsburgh. Driving me. Feeding me. Teaching me. Let me take care of you."

He looks at me. I look at him. The apartment is silent except for the hum of the refrigerator and the distant horn of a barge on the river.

He exhales long and shaky, accepting. "Come here."

I move from the coffee table to the couch, settling beside him on his uninjured side. He angles toward me, one hand coming up to cup my face, and kisses me. Slow at first, then deeper, his thumb tracing my jaw, and I taste the meatball sauce on his lip and feel the familiar rush of heat that Bernard's mouth generates in my bloodstream.

"Okay," he says against my lips. "Lesson."

"Lesson."

"You ever touch a wiener before?"

"Bernard! Wiener?" I laugh as his thumb rubs along my neck.

He smiles, so adorable. "I take it that's a no?"

I arch a brow. "Not one I wanted to put in my mouth."

He laughs the private Bernard laugh that cracks open his whole face. "Okay. Great, well, a penis is pretty straightforward. There's really no way you're going to be bad at this."

I glance down, and his crotch twitches under my gaze. He's quiet as he reaches into his waistband and pulls his shorts down. That thick, beautiful cock springs out at full attention, looking absolutely incredible and, yeah. Delicious. I decide I'm going to take him into my mouth, not just stroke him to completion.

He guides me. Verbally at first — what to do with my hand, how to grip, where the sensitive spots are. His voice is steady, instructional, the same tone he uses when quizzing me. I start with my hand around him, learning the shape and weight of him, the way his breathing changes when I adjust pressure.

"That's — yeah." His head tips back against the couch. "A little tighter. So good."

I pay attention, focused. Bernard makes sounds that send shock waves through my pajama pants, and his hand flaps on my shoulder like he is seizing. I bend at the waist, stick out my tongue, and taste the salty tip of his dick where the foreskin retracted. He emits a noise, and it's so hot I know I'll never forget the sound. Same with the groan from the night he climbed into bed with me. I glide my fist down and swirl the flat of my tongue around his tip.

"Ella — fuck — you don't—"

"Teach me," I say, and he moans. I don't wait for instruction. I somehow know what to do here, with Bernard's cock in my mouth. I want to make this man feel what he made me feel, to draw those sounds from him, to make his face contort in pleasure. And I see now how very good it feels to make someone else feel good.

I lower my mouth around his shaft and feel the gentle weight of his palm on my head, his fingers in my hair. I glance up and see his composure is gone. His hips jut up from the cushions. His face is a mess, neck tendons flexed. It's the most erotic thing … I'm overcome with an urge to touch myself.

I like this. I like the power of it. I like that Bernard Houser, who has been so controlled, so careful, so focused on my pleasure, is coming apart under my hands and my mouth. I like that I'm doing this to him. I slide a hand down the front of my pants just to take the pressure off while I work.

His voice is a sob. "Ella, I'm going to—you should—"

I don't pull away. I want this. I want to taste him, feel him shoot into my mouth. And oh, he does. He comes with my name on his lips and his hand clenched in my hair and an expression on his face that I have seen only once before, in the window of the aerial studio, when I looked up in triumph and felt, for the first time, powerful.

He's breathing hard. His eyes are closed. I swallow and release his still-hard cock. His hand loosens in my hair and slides down to my cheek, cradling my face with a tenderness that almost undoes me.

"Where the hell did you learn that?" he whispers.

"You just taught me."

"I taught you some basics. That was not a 101 blowie."

I sit up, wiping my mouth, trying to look composed and probably failing. "I told you. I'm a fast learner when someone teaches me the right way."

He pulls me against his side, careful of his knee, and wraps his arm around me. I tuck my head against his chest and listen to his heart — slowing, the percussion of a man returning to baseline. My hand rests on his stomach. His hand rests in my hair.

Neither of us says anything about tutoring. Neither of us mentions the right guy.

"Your ice pack needs swapping," I eventually murmur against his chest.

"In a minute."

"In a minute it'll have been too long."

"Ella."

"What?"

"Just ... stay here for now."

His heart beats against my ear. His fingers trace slow circles on my shoulder. The apartment is warm and dark and quiet, and it feels, for one dangerous moment, like home.

CHAPTER 14
HOWIE

My father has called four times today.

I've ignored all of them, despite having absolutely nothing to do apart from my PT homework exercises. Between those and staring at the ceiling thinking about Ella's lips, I've been very busy.

Too busy to talk to that guy, anyway.

I managed to get myself to and from the fridge for meals, and even ordered in some non-meatball food I plan to share with Ella when she gets home from work. I don't want to stop thinking about her tongue on me last night, the look in her eyes as she wrapped that mouth around my dick.

I've just situated myself back on the couch after tipping the delivery guy and setting food on the counter when a few things happen at once. First, my phone rings again, the word DAD flashing across the screen. Then the apartment door opens, and even though it's dark outside, the condo fills with light as Ella walks in with a smile on her face.

So yeah, I'm not talking to my dad right now, while I could be looking at her instead. I don't even fucking care about the consequences anymore. I silence the phone and toss it on the rug as Ella sinks onto the couch, kicking off her clogs with a groan.

"Long day?" I shift my weight so my body is angled toward hers. The phone buzzes again.

"It was intense. Multi-car crash on the parkway. Do you have to take that?" She gestures at my phone with one hand and starts rubbing her foot with the other.

I stare at her hands, kneading the flesh of her sole. "It's my dad just calling to reiterate his bullshit."

She arches a brow. "He's delusional."

I nod. Ella knows my dad rides me hard. Wouldn't take me to a specialist for my shoulder in high school, so I needed that first surgery the summer before freshman year. "Just because he played with a torn rotator cuff and a broken hand doesn't mean that's my formula for longevity in the league."

Ella winces. "It's such a shitty thing to pressure you about anyway. Your medical staff wouldn't clear you, would they?"

I shake my head. "Try telling Howie Houser, senior, that things have changed since his glory days."

Her nose wrinkles adorably. "Glory days? Didn't he get suspended for a cheap shot that almost broke someone's neck?"

I nod. She's not the only one walking in a hockey player's shadow. Coaches and league officials all remember my old man. Other players, once they put it together, treat me like I'm going to act the same way. I confess, "Everyone treats me with caution, like I'm going to be violent."

"You're nothing like him." She drops a hand to my arm and squeezes for emphasis.

"You don't know that."

"Bernard." Her fingers thread through mine. "You are nothing like a man who hits people from behind."

My throat tightens. I look at our hands — mine huge, scarred across the knuckles from a decade of blocked shots, hers smaller, a little chapped from work, strong. We fit together in a way that makes me feel invincible. I cough and point at the counter, trying to defuse the situation. "I got us food from Nicky's Thai."

Her face lights up even brighter, and she's on her feet in a flash, gathering bags. The aroma of garlic and ginger wafts toward me, and my mouth waters as she pulls out containers and wooden chopsticks. "What's all in here?"

———

Ella rushed through a shower while the fried spring rolls cooled, and then we dug into a feast on the couch. We've just finished demolishing pad Thai, rice curry, and mango salad when my phone rings again. I kick it with my good foot, and it skitters across the floor, under the television.

She stares at it. "Feel better?"

I grunt. "Not really."

"I know that ache," she says, placing our empty containers on the floor before settling back into the cushions. "The parent thing. Feeling like no matter what you accomplish, it's never the right accomplishment."

"Your parents had a script for you, too?"

"My parents had a script for Jason. I wasn't even in the cast." She shrugs. "Different flavor of the same thing. You're seen as the wrong version of yourself. I'm not seen at all."

I look at her. She looks at me. The apartment is dark except for the TV glow and the lamp she always leaves on, the one by the curtains, and her face is half-lit and half-shadow, and I think: she doesn't need lessons.

She's never needed lessons. This woman cracks me open, and she does it without trying, without technique, without any of the bullshit I've been pretending to teach her.

Ella Rujkowski is better at intimacy than anyone I've ever been with. She just doesn't know it. She thinks she's inexperienced. She thinks she needs training. But the things she does...I've never had this with anyone else.

She runs her fingers through my hair. Slow, the way she learned I like, nails dragging gently across my scalp. My eyes close. The tension in my shoulders loosens. Her nail traces the scar in my eyebrow, and I feel my body respond — not just arousal, though that's there, instant and undeniable — but something deeper. A release. A surrender.

"You don't need lessons," I murmur.

Her hand pauses. "What?"

"You heard me." I open my eyes. "You touch me all the right ways and say the right things, and I come apart. You don't need a single lesson, Ella. Your brother is the only obstacle between you and any man alive falling at your feet."

She stares at me. Her hand resumes its seduction in my hair, slower now, and I can see her processing, filing that statement, testing its weight.

"I still want you," she says. Simple. Direct.

"I still want you too. That's been pretty well established."

"I mean tonight." Her eyes hold mine.

My heart rate does something the team doctor would flag. "Ella—"

"I know what I'm asking." She pulls her hand from my hair and places it on my chest, palm flat, the way she did that first time on the couch when she felt my heartbeat and realized I wasn't calm. "Is your knee too painful?"

"My knee is ..." I glance down at it. Wrapped, elevated, aching in the background, the way it has been for days. "It depends on the position."

"What position feels best?"

I swallow. "If you were on top. That would ... my knee wouldn't be bearing weight. And I could..." I stop and try to concentrate. "Having you on top would be incredibly hot, Ella. I want to see you. Your body. Your face."

Something passes across her features. A shadow I've seen before, when she crossed her arms over her bare chest, when she commented on being too big to sit on my lap. The cruel voice in her head that says she takes up too much space.

"I'm not exactly light," she says.

"Ella." I sit up straighter, ignoring the protest from my knee. "Look at me."

She looks.

"You could sit on me right now, and the only thing I'd feel is lucky. I have wanted your full weight on me since I saw you at the airport. I have thought about nothing else. Do you understand? You on top of me is not a compromise because of my knee. It's a fucking fantasy."

Her cheeks flush. Her eyes go bright. She bites that bottom lip, and I watch her face shift from doubt to something that looks like hunger.

"I should tell you something," I say, because apparently I've lost all self-preservation instinct. "I think about you when I touch myself. In the shower. Every time. Since before the first *lesson*. I think about your body and your sounds and your face when you come, and I," I exhale. "That's not tutoring."

She's quiet for a beat, then says, "I think about you too."

"Yeah?"

"In your bed. At night. After you fall asleep on the couch." She holds my gaze. "I hear you breathing through the wall, and I think about your hands, and I touch myself, and I pretend it's you."

Every drop of blood in my body swims south. My vision narrows to her face, her mouth, the flush spreading down her neck beneath her scrubs. I can picture it, Ella in my bed, in the dark, her hand between her thighs, my name in her mouth, and I'm so hard it strains against my shorts.

"Show me," I say, and my voice comes out wrecked. "Please. I want to see. I want to see how you touch yourself, Ella. Get on top of me and show me how you get off."

She looks around, seeming uncomfortable. "Not on the couch."

"Wherever you want," I agree.

She helps me up, careful with the knee, slotting herself under my arm like she's done it a hundred times. We make our way down the hall — me limping, her steady — to the bedroom. Her bedroom. My bedroom. The room that smells like both of us now, the pillows she sleeps on, the space where she's been lying in the dark thinking about me.

She sits me on the edge of the bed, and I scoot back, propping my bad leg on a pillow. She stands in front of me and pulls her top over her head. The sports bra follows. Then the pajama pants, and she's standing there in underwear, and my mouth goes dry because it doesn't matter how many times I see her — every time hits me like Mayhem on dull skates. Except Ella is soft and strong and so beautiful, my chest aches.

She hooks her thumbs in her underwear. Pauses.

"Please, show me," I say.

She slides them down and steps out of them, and she's naked in front of me, and I'm looking at her like she's the only thing in the world because right now she is.

"Come here," I beg. "Please. Straddle me. I want to feel you."

She climbs onto the bed, swings a leg over my hips, and settles her weight onto me, and the pressure of her — the heat, the softness, the full gorgeous reality of Ella Rujkowski sitting on top of me — makes me groan so loud the neighbors probably hear it.

"Is this okay?" she asks. "Your knee—"

"My knee is perfect. Everything is perfect. You're perfect." I grip her hips with both hands, feeling the curve of her, the give of her skin under my fingers. "Show me, Ella. Show me what you do when you think about me."

I have zero concern for the fact that she's my roommate's

sister. Right now, she's the hottest woman in any universe, and she's naked for *me*. She reaches between us. Her fingers find the place she needs, and she starts to move — slow, tentative at first, her eyes half-closed — and I watch her face, and I hold her hips, and I think: this is it. This is the moment I can't come back from.

I don't just lust after Ella Rujkowski. I'm pretty sure I'm in love with her, and she's on top of me, and she's touching herself, and I'm about to be *inside* her. Nothing, not the tutoring, not the right guy, not her brother, not my father, none of it matters as much as the expression on her face right now.

She opens her eyes and looks down at me and says, "Bernard."

Her fingers flutter faster as she stares into my eyes.

I'm done for.

CHAPTER 15
ELLA

As I rock on top of Bernard, touching myself in ways that have always been private until now, one thought repeats itself: I want him.

Not as a tutor. Not as practice for some mythical "right guy," but just for himself. He's beneath me, his massive body solid and warm, eyes hooded, words so encouraging, and I want him.

My fingers circle and press in a rhythm I've used with Bernard on my mind, and nothing about this feels like practice. His hand grips my hip, an anchor. His eyes are dark, fixed on my face, filled with want.

Everything adult Bernard has done since I arrived in Pittsburgh has been in service of my safety and comfort. Rides to work. Actual interest in my studying drama. He says he thinks I'm capable, and I can feel the truth of that.

I look down at him, on the verge of coming, and the hunger on his face is real. Not performed or rehearsed.

"I want you inside me," I say.

His jaw tightens. "Are you sure?"

"I've never been more sure of anything."

I watch him swallow, feel his erection against my bottom

as I squirm on top of him. "Ella, I want you to be ready. So it doesn't hurt as much…"

"Right. Okay." I let my hand drop to his belly, feeling the skin of my thighs against his flanks.

His hands slide from my hips to my thighs, thumbs tracing slow circles on my inner skin. And then one thick finger presses inside me, slow, careful. I gasp, and his eyes flash, concerned. "Does that hurt?" His voice is rough with restraint.

"No. It's so good." The sensation is strange, full, and intimate.

He adds a second finger, and I moan —fuller now, a stretch that borders on too much before it settles into something warm and deep. His thumb finds my clit and begins to circle, and the combination of his fingers inside me and the pressure outside makes my vision blur at the edges.

"I'm going to make you feel so damn good, baby," he says, and the words are a promise and a prayer, and I believe him completely because Bernard Houser has never once broken a promise to me.

He works me with his hand — patient, attentive, reading my body the way he reads the ice, adjusting pressure and rhythm based on the sounds I make and the way my hips move. I brace my hands on his chest and let the wave build, let it crest, and when I come this time, it's deeper than before, a full-body pulse that makes me clench around his fingers and cry out his name.

He holds me through it. Steady. Solid. His other hand on my hip, grounding me while I shake. I feel my belly against his, soft against solid, but I'm too far gone in pleasure to worry that he might not like the sensation.

"God, Ella," he whispers. "You're incredible."

I'm still trembling when he reaches toward the nightstand. The drawer slides open, and I look over. And then I start to laugh.

There must be forty condoms in there. A chaotic pile of foil packets in every brand and variety, crammed into the drawer like a pharmacy exploded.

"Oh my god, Bernard."

"In my defense, these were here before you moved in." He rummages through the pile and holds up a blue packet with silver lettering. "Not these. Definitely not these."

I squint at the label. THIN ICE. "What's wrong with 'defense never felt so good'?"

Bernard laughs beneath me, his muscles flexing in a way that soothes me and sets me even more at ease. "Tucker Stag endorsed those until they didn't work, and now he has twins."

A full-body shudder runs through me. I might be experiencing big feelings today, but the desire for motherhood is not among them. "Put those in the trash."

"Gladly." He tosses the Thin Ice packet across the room and produces a regular condom and a small foil packet of lube. "These are the good ones."

I take the condom from him. My hands shake slightly as I tear the wrapper. I scoot back further down his legs, feeling the hair on his thighs tickle my bottom. He watches me, patient, and when I fumble the first attempt, he covers my hands with his and guides me, rolling it down his length, slow, together.

His cock is massive, erect, with skin so taut it's like suede over a hot iron. I want to taste it again. I am about to have this inside my body.

"Now the lube," he says. "Just…yeah, drizzle it. Make me slick."

I tear the lube packet and spread it over him, and the slide of my hand on the condom makes him groan and thrust into my fist. He's hard, thick, and ready, and I'm terrified, desperate, and certain all at once.

"Whenever you're ready," he says. "Your pace. You're in control."

I brace my hands on his shoulders. His hands settle on my hips. I rise on my knees, position him beneath me, and begin to lower myself down.

He slides into me like he was meant to be there. "We're doing it," I exclaim, and I laugh along with him.

"Yeah, we are, Ella. Fuuuuck."

I freeze halfway, breathing, adjusting. There's a stretch — not quite pain but not quite comfort, the feeling of my body making room for something it hasn't held before. Bernard's hands tighten on my hips, but he doesn't move. He waits. His eyes search my face.

"Okay?" he whispers.

"Yeah."

I sink lower. Inch by inch. The stretch becomes fullness, and the fullness becomes something I don't have a word for—connection, maybe, or completeness, or the feeling of a lock clicking into place. My body takes him in, and I rest there, seated fully, and I feel so close to him, so full of so many things.

"Ella." His voice cracks. "You feel — fuck — you feel—"

"I know."

I start to move. Slow at first, rocking my hips, finding a rhythm that works with his injured leg and my inexperienced body. His hands guide me, not directing, just steadying, letting me find my own pace while his hips rise gently to meet mine.

His mouth finds my breast. Lips and tongue on my nipple, and the dual sensation of him inside me and his wet mouth draws moans from me so loud, I'm grateful the condo is empty.

"Oh my god," he breathes against my skin. "Ella, look at you. You're so fucking beautiful, do you know that? Do you have any idea..."

I roll my hips harder. His hands grip tighter, sinking into the soft cushion of my backside. The rhythm builds, and I find it: the angle, the pressure, the pace that makes everything tighten and climb. "I think I might come again, Bernard," I whisper.

His eyes are molten. I see the drive there, the professional athlete attuned to his task, which is apparently destroying me with orgasms. His hips thrust up off the bed to meet mine, and the sound of our bodies together fills the bedroom.

"Christ," he groans, and his eyes are locked on my chest, watching me move above him, watching my breasts bounce with each thrust. "You are a goddamn masterpiece. Every inch of you. I can't — Ella — I can't believe—"

His praise pours over me like warm water. I take what I need. I brace my hands on his shoulders and ride him, and I feel powerful in a way that has nothing to do with silks or nursing or passing a test. I feel powerful because Bernard Houser is looking at me like I'm the sun and he's been living in the dark.

I cannot imagine anything ever feeling this incredible. His body under mine, his hands on my hips, his mouth worshipping my skin. It's everything. It's all I want.

I come a third time, and this one breaks me open. I feel it in my spine, in my fingers, in the roots of my hair. I clench around him, and he groans my name and thrusts up hard, once, twice, and I watch his face as he comes, too.

I was not expecting to love this sight so much.

His eyes close. His mouth falls open. His neck arches and his hands go rigid on my hips, and the expression on his face is the most beautiful thing I have ever seen. Open. Unguarded. Trusting. He looks the way I feel, like every wall is down, every performance abandoned. Just Bernard. Real and raw and mine.

The word arrives without permission: *mine*.

I look at his face, the openness there, the trust he shows me, and I return, and I realize with the calm certainty of a nurse reading vitals that I am probably in love with Bernard Houser.

Our breathing slows. I lift off him carefully, both of us wincing at the separation, and roll onto my side next to him. He pulls me close immediately, arm around my waist, tucking me against his chest. His heart hammers against my cheek.

We lie there. His hand moves in slow circles on my back. My hand rests on his stomach, feeling it rise and fall. The bedroom is dark and warm and quiet, and I don't want to move, but I do know we can't leave a condom situation unattended.

"Stay," I tell him. "I'll be right back."

I clean up in the bathroom, where a look in the mirror reveals a woman I barely recognize. Flushed. Bright-eyed. Wrecked in the best way. I bring a washcloth and the small trash can from the bathroom back to the bed. Bernard cleans up, ties off the condom, and tosses it while I crawl back under the covers beside him.

"Bernard?"

"Mm."

"Will you sleep in here tonight? With me?"

He laughs, low and tired and happy. "Ella, there is absolutely no way I could move from this bed right now, even if the building were on fire."

"Is that a yes?"

"That's a yes."

I press against his side, tuck my head into the curve of his shoulder, and feel his arm tighten around me. His lips brush my forehead. His breathing deepens.

The last time Bernard Houser was in this bed with me, it was an accident. He stumbled in drunk and grabbed me in his sleep, and I lay there in the dark feeling the ghost of his arm around my waist, wondering what it would be like to be held on purpose.

Now I know.

It feels safe.

I THOUGHT SIGNING WITH THE FURY WAS THE HAPPIEST I'D EVER be, but turns out living with Ella Rujkowski, and just getting to be with her, is way better.

We took things to the next level last night, and today, when Ella comes home from her shift, I wait for her in bed. She climbs in beside me like we've always slept together, and we make out for a while before she falls asleep with her head on my chest. I lie there with the solid weight of her on me, and her breath against my collarbone, and I think: I could do this forever.

———

Ella sits on my lap wearing only my jersey. It's hot as fuck, but I told her she can't come until she passes a practice quiz. I'm not sure I'm going to make it. She's on a roll, though, eyes pinched shut in concentration while I touch her everywhere except her clit. She gets every question right while I tell her she's brilliant. Her cheeks flush, and she bites back a smile along with a moan when I let the side of my thumb graze her swollen little nub. After she nails the last question, I slam the laptop shut, and she jams a condom on me so fast. We fuck right there on the couch, with her on top again, nipples poking out through the material of my shirt. She comes twice with my hand between us, and I watch her face because I'm collecting these expressions like some kids store up hockey cards.

————

Ella has the day off, and I don't have PT. We stay in the bedroom until the skin on my cock is sore. She sits cross-legged on the mattress, naked, while we recite drug interactions. I lick every inch of her body, and then I eat Thai food off her stomach while she shrieks that the noodles are cold.

After I lap up the last drop of sauce, she grabs me by the hair and says, "You're actually a St. Bernard, aren't you? Big and drooly, taking up the whole bed?"

"I'm sorry, but did you just compare me to a dog?" I splay a hand across her belly, finger jiggling her boobs.

She laughs. "I did. A dog that rescues people." And nobody has ever thought of me as a savior. I have to be inside her, and I manage to be on top without too much discomfort in my knee.

————

The Fury physical therapist says my knee is progressing well. I'm almost at full flexion, and Anya says I could be skating again in a week.

When I get back to the condo, Ella is there, and I tell her the news, and she whoops. "We need to celebrate. I aced three practice tests in a row, so we've both had great days." She stands in her socks and does a little shimmy that instantly makes me hard.

I tip my head toward the bedroom, and she giggles—giggles! The next thing I know, we're both in the shower with her bent over, clutching the built-in bench seat, and me standing behind her, thrusting slow and deep while the water pours over us. The urge to tell her I love her is powerful, but the smile on her face is distracting, and after we both come, we kiss until the water runs cold.

———

Friday, I come back from PT, and she's still at work. I notice her suitcase in the corner of the bedroom, still packed. Like she's five weeks into a hotel stay rather than living somewhere. I hate it.

I do a quick inventory of my dresser and decide I can put my socks and underwear in one drawer so Ella can at least have one to herself. Women need space for private things. Everyone does.

While I'm at it, I rearrange the closet so it's half empty, and I steal a bunch of hangers from Rookie's room so that when she comes home, she sees the space as an invitation to stay as long as she wants.

I station myself on the couch and act engrossed in the game on TV when Ella gets home from work. "Hey, B," she trills, a new nickname that has my nerve endings fizzing in happiness. I wave and stay put while she heads into the room to change. I hear her pause, imagine her taking in the gesture. And then I hear the sounds of suitcase zippers and pants being shaken onto hangers.

I limp to the bedroom and lean against the door frame, watching. She turns to me, a dress clutched against her chest and a smile splitting her face. "Did you do all this?"

I nod. "Cleared out the top drawer for you, too, if you want." I lean into the room and flick it open, gesturing at the open space.

A tiny tear forms at the corner of her eye, and she brushes it away, smiling. Ella bends to grab a bundle of stuff from her suitcase and sets it in the drawer without saying a word.

"Bro. You good?" Rookie drops his road bag in the hallway and stares at me.

I'm on the couch, knee wrapped, watching film from the road games I missed. Ella is at work. The apartment is clean. The drawer is full of her clothes, and the closet has her shoes, and none of this is visible from the living room, but I still feel like I'm wearing a confession.

"I've been doing PT," I say. "Getting healthy."

"You look … rested." He squints. "Did you sleep?"

"On occasion."

He collapses onto the couch beside me, long legs sprawling, and starts scrolling his phone. "We went one and two. Spinner had a hat trick in Carolina, though. You should have seen it." He launches into a play-by-play, complete with hand gestures and sound effects, and I listen because these are my teammates and it's my job to know this stuff.

Rookie's energy and volume fill the room. I used to be the same way. The life of the party. The loud one. Now I'm sitting here thinking about how Ella fell asleep with her head on my chest, and I don't want to be loud anymore. I want to be quiet with her.

"We should go out," Rookie announces. "You've been cooped up in here for a week. Get some real food. Gianna's?"

"I don't know, man. My knee—"

"You can put your leg on a bench. Come on. I'll text the guys."

I should say no. I should stay on this couch and wait for Ella and preserve what little remains of this bubble. But saying no to Rookie right now, when he's looking at me with that oblivious golden retriever enthusiasm, would raise questions I can't answer.

"Fine," I say. "Meatballs sound great."

Gianna's is crowded. The back room is ours, per usual, though, and I have my leg propped up on a bench next to Spinner while Mayhem reads something on his phone and Jason inhales dry turkey meatballs like he's been starved the whole week.

Other guys filter in and out. Cappy and Banksy stop by. Even Grentley makes an appearance, drinks a single beer in the corner like a vampire at a cookout, and leaves without saying goodbye to anyone.

The beers flow my way from all the guys. Gianna keeps them coming, and I'm on my fourth when Rookie tells a story about a fan in Florida who asked him to sign her chest, and he accidentally drew a dick.

"It wasn't accidental," Spinner says.

"It was! My hand slipped!"

"Your hand drew a full shaft with veins, Rookie."

The table erupts. I'm laughing, loose, warm. My knee doesn't hurt. The food is good. My friends are here. For a minute, I forget the weight I'm carrying, and I'm just Howie — life of the party, the one who makes sure everyone has a good time.

Rookie looks at me with glassy eyes. "We—" he hiccups. "Should not drive home, and you can't walk with that knee, bruh."

I shake my head. "That is correct."

"Hey," he says, pulling out his phone. "Ella can come pick up your car. Save the dishwashers a trip." Warning bells ring in my foggy head, but he's already texting. "She's off tonight, right?"

"I think so," I manage, because my throat just closed. I know exactly when her shift ends, and which route she'll take to get here from Mercy. Maybe she'll bring her friends to flirt with Spinner again.

"Cool. I told her to meet us here, and she can drive your G-Wagon home." He pockets his phone, satisfied with himself. "See? I care about people."

"That's … great, Rook."

Spinner orders another round. Mayhem closes whatever he's reading and folds his hands on the table. I have another beer. This is a mistake. I know it's a bad idea while I'm drinking it, but the alternative is sitting here sober while Ella walks through that door and pretending she's just my roommate's sister, and I don't have the playbook for that right now.

Eventually, the door opens, and cold air sweeps in, and there she is.

She's in jeans and a sweater, hair down, and she looks soft and happy and so beautiful that the sight of her hits me like a stick to the jaw. My head snaps back just as hard. She scans the room, finds our table, and smiles, a polite, public expression, one that isn't for me.

Except it is for me. It's always for me now. I see the real thing underneath, the private warmth, the way her eyes linger on my face for half a second longer than they should.

"Hey guys," she says, dropping into the chair Spinner pulls out for her. "Jason said you need a designated driver."

"Just us roomies," Rookie says, playfully punching her shoulder. "These other fuckers can get themselves home."

"Hi, Ella." Spinner raises his glass. "How's circus school?"

"Still not a circus. Hi, Mayhem."

Mayhem nods. Watches.

Gianna brings a plate of food to Ella without being asked, and Ella thanks her. I watch her eat a meatball, and I remember Tuesday on the couch and her victory shimmy in socks and the sound she makes when I'm inside her and her clothes in my drawer, and I am six beers deep, and my chest is too full, and my brain is too slow, and she's RIGHT THERE.

She reaches across me for a napkin. Her sweater brushes my arm. I smell her body wash — the fruity one, the one that lives on my pillow now — and something in my drunk, demolished brain just ... stops working.

I catch her wrist. Pull her toward me. Cup the back of her neck with my other hand and kiss her.

Not a peck. Not a friendly thing. I kiss her the way I kiss her in the dark in our bedroom, deep and slow and sure, and for approximately two seconds the world is perfect because her mouth is on mine and her hand grabs my shirt and I feel her soften against me before—

She pulls back. Fast. Laughing.

"Okay, big guy." She pats my chest and gives me a push, her voice pitched for the table. "Someone's had enough." She turns to her brother, still laughing, steady as a trauma nurse. "How many has he had?"

"Too damn many," Rookie says, white-knuckling his grip on a beer bottle. "Dude, did you just kiss my sister?"

"He kissed Spinner on the Fourth of July," Gianna offers from behind the bar.

"That's true," Spinner confirms, eyeing Gianna in a familiar way. "I have very soft lips."

The table laughs. Rookie rolls his eyes. The moment passes, absorbed into the noise of Saturday night at Gianna's, filed under "Howie got drunk and sloppy," which is a category with extensive precedent.

Ella settles in on the bench and eats another meatball and doesn't look at me. Her hand, beneath the table, finds my thigh and squeezes once. Hard. A message: *you absolute idiot*.

Fair.

Gianna comes by to collect keys, and Rookie waves her off. "Ella's driving."

The night winds down. Spinner tells two more stories.

Rookie arm-wrestles Cappy and loses. Ella chats with Banksy and Cam, who apparently know about some charity event they want her involved with. She's charming and easy, and nobody watching her would ever guess that she spent the week with my cock inside her while I said things about her body that would make a priest faint.

I'm gathering myself to stand when I feel the weight of a stare. Mayhem.

His arms are crossed, and his face is neutral, but his eyes say everything. This isn't the "be careful" from the bar two weeks ago. This is past careful. This is: I know.

I hold his gaze. He holds mine. The noise of the restaurant fades to static.

He shakes his head.

Then he stands, drops cash on the table, and leaves without a word.

CHAPTER 17
ELLA

I'm a person who has sex. Lots of sex.

Except it's all been with someone I should not bang.

Last night, I thought the world was going to swallow me whole when Bernard kissed me not only in front of my brother but with half his teammates there to witness. I got the sense that some of the guys knew more than they let on when they jumped in with explanations, but Jason eventually seemed to buy the fact that Bernard was drunk, and apparently gets real affectionate when he hits the sauce.

I lie still for a minute, alone in Bernard's bed, staring at the closet where my clothes now hang beside his. The drawer he cleared for me is full. My shoes are lined up next to his. From this angle, the room looks like two people live in it, which is a problem because only one of us is supposed to.

I shower, dress, and emerge to find Jason at the kitchen counter shoveling eggs into his mouth while scrolling his phone. Bernard is on the couch with his knee elevated, watching highlights. They look like two guys sharing an apartment. Normal. Fine.

I'm back to being an intruder in their bachelor lives.

Bernard glances at me when I enter the kitchen. Nothing on his face but casual friendliness. "Morning."

"Morning." I pour coffee and sit on the stool, and ... we are two people who had sex in every room of this apartment and are now performing polite distance over mugs of French roast.

Jason talks about today's practice schedule. I nod, eat a banana, and feel Bernard's presence in the room like a frequency only I can hear.

I leave for my shift without touching him. Without looking at him longer than a roommate would. I walk to the elevator with my jaw clenched and my chest tight, and I think: this is how it has to be.

The texting starts at noon.

BERNARD

This couch is a crime against humanity.

BERNARD

It's a $10,000 torture device, and it smells like my sadness.

ME

Dramatic much?

BERNARD

I woke up at 3 am and almost walked to the bedroom.

I stare at that message. My thumb hovers. I type and delete three responses before settling on:

ME

We need to talk about rules.

BERNARD

I know.

ME

Tonight? When Jason goes to sleep?

BERNARD
We've got a game tonight. It'll be late.

ME
I don't work tomorrow. I can stay up so we can figure this out.

I pocket my phone and press my palms against my eyes. Figure this out. Like, there's a protocol. Why aren't there protocols for people like there are for assessing trauma patients?

————————

I walk home from work today, since the weather is decent and I've got a lot on my mind. It occurs to me that I could go to the guys' games. Shouldn't one of them put tickets aside for me or something? In a fantasy world, Bernard would get me seats right on the blue line, and I'd wear his jersey like I did the last time we had sex on the couch.

My cheeks heat at the memory, both because he made me come so many times and because I really like spending time with the guy I used to pray would disappear from the back-seat of my parents' car.

At home, I change into sweats, make myself a sandwich, and study at the counter until I hear keys in the lock.

Jason's voice arrives before he does, whooping. "Did you see me give that Buffalo asshole a face wash? Man, I'm amped up for another go at them tomorrow."

Bernard enters the room, and his eyes snap directly to me, revealing an anxious expression before he slides on a mask of indifference as my brother squeezes past him en route to the snack cupboard. "Ellie-belly, you haven't been hitting my jerky, have you? We talked about this."

I groan. "I have a negative desire to eat your elk parts, Jason."

He holds up a stick of dehydrated meat like a pointer. "Just checking. I'm hitting the sack." His door slams and rock music blasts, slightly muffled, moments later.

This means Bernard and I are alone for the moment. I close the laptop and walk over to where he's seated stiffly on the couch, still wearing the suit he must have put on to watch the game from the stands. "Hey."

"Hey." He starts loosening his tie.

"So." I tap my hands on my thighs.

"So."

I tuck my feet under me and face him. "We need ground rules. For when Jason's home."

He pulls off his belt and sets it on the coffee table. "Okay."

"No touching. Not in common areas, not where he could walk in."

"Okay."

"No lingering looks. No inside jokes he can't follow. No calling me anything that isn't my name."

"I only ever call you your name."

"You called me *baby* the other night." I press my legs together at the memory of my body's response to hearing him call me that, like a treasured, precious thing.

Something flickers across his face. He remembers. "That was ... a heat of the moment thing."

"It was a nice heat-of-the-moment thing. But not when Jason's around."

"Okay," he repeats, and his voice is flat. Not angry. Just drained. Like I'm reading him a list of things he's lost.

"Bernard."

"I'm fine with the rules, Ella. They make sense."

"But?"

He rubs the back of his neck. Stares at the curtains he hung. "No buts. You're right. This is smart."

He means it. I can tell he does. But I can also tell that something in him is folding inward, a door closing that was wide open five days ago, and I don't know how to keep it ajar without risking everything.

A long time passes before he speaks. Finally, he gestures at the laptop on the counter. "You want me to quiz you? Your boards are coming up."

We study. Side by side on the couch, a careful eight inches between us. He asks me about pharmacokinetics, and I answer correctly, and he says "good" in his normal voice, and I miss the playfulness he shows so often when we're alone.

After I ace a bunch of questions, I go to bed. I lie in the dark and hear Bernard settling onto the couch, hear the leather squeak as he shifts, trying to find a position that doesn't hurt his knee.

My phone glows.

BERNARD

Goodnight, Ella.

ME

Goodnight.

I press the phone against my chest and close my eyes.

———

I'm halfway through a shift, a few days later, when my phone starts going wild in my pocket.

I've been added to some sort of group chat titled FURY PAWS 🐾 🔥, and the first message I see is:

CAM

WELCOME ELLA!! The partners and wives are so excited to meet you properly

ESSENCE

Hi babe!! Cappy said you were at Gianna's on Saturday. SO glad you're settling in Pittsburgh!

CAM

We heard someone got a kiss at the meatball joint •• 🔥

My stomach drops through the floor.

ESSENCE

Spill immediately

I type fast, thumbs clumsy on the screen.

ME

Ha, no, that was just Howie being drunk. I'm Jason's sister, that's all. Howie kisses everyone when he's wasted, apparently.

CAM

LOL that tracks. Howie kissed Banksy at a charity event last year, and Banksy still talks about it.

ESSENCE

Girl, either way, you are one of us now. Next home game, you're sitting with us. No arguments.

EMERSON

Hi Ella! I'm Emerson, Gunnar's wife. Welcome to the group 💜 These folks saved my life when I moved to Pittsburgh.

LENA

Lena here — team dentist (and Alder's partner, hi). So which Fury guy should we set you up with? We've got options 😏

My heart hammers at the speed with which I lost control of this situation. I just wanted someone to have sex with me so I would know what it felt like. And, my traitorous brain reminds me, I kept on having sex with that person because he turned out to be incredible.

ME

Haha, no guys needed! Just here to study for my nursing boards and cheer on my brother. Thanks for the warm welcome though 🙏

CAM

Ok, but if you change your mind, we have OPINIONS

ESSENCE

Strong opinions

EMERSON

Very strong. Welcome, Ella 🖤

I lock my phone, lean against the wall, and breathe. These folks are warm and welcoming and funny, and they just invited me into the inner circle of Fury life, and all I can think is: will my brother's rules take this from me? These friendly people in my life, paired with the amazing physical stuff I've been doing with Bernard…it all feels so vibrant and addictive. I'm worried it will all slip away, like most things I yearn for.

———————

Saturday morning, Aarthi picks me up in the Honda Civic. The READY TO WED bumper sticker now has a sticky note over it that says NOT READY — STOP ASKING, which Aarthi claims her mother hasn't noticed yet.

McKenzie is in the back with coffees and a resistance band she's been using to "pre-game" for silks. "I watched YouTube tutorials all week," she announces. "I can almost do a basic inversion."

"I pulled a muscle brushing my teeth this morning," Aarthi says. "So we're at different levels."

The studio is busier this time — more women, a few regulars who nod at us as we belong. Jules remembers our names.

We warm up, stretch, and I feel the familiar burn in my shoulders as I grip the silk and start to climb.

I'm better this week. Stronger. My foot lock clicks into place on the first try, and I hold it, suspended, reaching for the next grip. My body remembers what my brain learned last time, and the muscle memory feels like a revelation, proof that I can learn things when the format is right.

McKenzie nails an inversion and cheers so loud that Jules has to shush her. Aarthi manages a full climb and descends with a controlled grace that surprises all of us, including Aarthi. I work on transitions from the foot lock, leaning back, extending, and finding shapes in the silk that feel like mine.

After class, we sprawl on the mats, sweaty and raw-handed, passing around a water bottle.

"So," McKenzie says. "Are you okay?"

I look at her. "What?"

"You seem off." She rolls onto her side, facing me. "Like your body's here but your brain is in another zip code."

"I'm fine."

Aarthi sits up. "Your 'fine' has a very specific look, and it's the same one you had when you failed that practice test."

"I didn't fail anything. I actually scheduled my real boards." I say this brightly, realizing this is a big deal I should have led with when they picked me up. "February twenty-ninth. Lucky Leap Day, right?"

McKenzie claps. "That's huge! Ella! I love that you're doing it on Leap Day."

"We should celebrate," Aarthi says. "That's major."

"It's terrifying, is what it is."

"It's both." McKenzie studies me. "But that's not what's eating you. Is it the roommate situation?"

My throat tightens. "What do you mean?"

"We're all stressed about work, but you seem extra... agitated," Aarthi says gently. "I'm sensing a vibe."

I laugh despite myself. "I just ... need space from my

brother. Living with Jason is a lot. He's loud, and he's everywhere, and I can't ..." I trail off. Regroup. "I need my own life. I need to pass this test so I can get a real paycheck, find my own place, and just be Ella. Not Baby Rookie. Not someone's sister."

They nod. McKenzie squeezes my arm. Aarthi bumps her shoulder against mine.

"You're already Ella to us," McKenzie says. "Have been since day one."

I smile, and it's real, but it's not the whole truth. The whole truth is that it's not Jason I've gotten too close to in that apartment. It's not my brother's shadow I'm struggling to escape anymore.

It's Bernard's gravity. The pull of him.

I need to pass this test. I need my own apartment. I need to figure out what this thing with Bernard is before it figures itself out in the worst possible way.

I roll off the mat, lace up my shoes, and follow my friends into the cold Pittsburgh morning.

MAYHEM CORNERS ME IN THE TRAINING ROOM.

I'm on the bike, rehabbing my knee, headphones in, trying not to think about the fact that Ella left for work this morning without touching me, for the sixth day in a row.

He sits on the bench across from me and waits. Just sits there with his hands on his knees, filling the room with his six-foot-five silence until I pull out an earbud.

"What?"

"Get off the bike."

"I have twelve more minutes."

"Come on, Howie."

I obey, and he hands me a towel while I swig from my water bottle. We sit in the training room while the rest of the guys run drills above us, the thud of pucks and the scrape of blades filtering through the ceiling.

Mayhem takes his time, as per usual. He's fast as fuck on skates, but very much the silent observer on our shenanigans. "I'm going to say something," he says, finally. "And you're going to listen."

"Okay."

"You're in love with Rookie's sister."

My brows shoot up, and I open my mouth to deny it, to

deflect, to make a joke about how Mayhem's been reading too much, but nothing comes out. Because he's right.

"I'm not going to lecture you," he says. "You're a grown man. She's a grown woman. I don't care who you sleep with."

"But."

"But Rookie doesn't know. And the longer he doesn't know, the worse it gets." He leans forward, elbows on his knees. "You think you're protecting him. Or protecting her. Or protecting yourself. But what you're actually doing is building a bomb. Need I remind you what happened with Grentley and T Stag?"

I stare at the floor. The tile is scuffed and stained with years of athletic tape residue and spilled Gatorade.

"Tell Rook," Mayhem says. "Before he finds out. Because if he finds out on his own, it won't matter that you love her. All he'll hear is that you lied."

"I know."

"Do you? Because I watched you kiss her in front of the whole team and then let her pretend it was nothing. That's careless."

The word lands. The thing everyone already thinks I am. The party boy. The yes man. The guy who can't say no to temptation.

"I'm going to tell him," I say.

"When?"

"After her boards. She takes the NCLEX soon, and she's stressed enough. I don't want to blow up her life right before—"

"There's always a reason to wait." Mayhem stands. Looks down at me. "But silence can cut deeper than truth sometimes."

He leaves. The door clicks shut, and I sit on the bench with my towel and my water bottle and the echo of the truest thing anyone has said to me in weeks.

Practice ends, and I'm in the recovery pool when my phone buzzes on the deck. I grab it with a wet hand, expecting Ella.

It's a link from Spinner. A podcast clip. The message says:

> heads up, bro.

I click it, and my father's voice fills the room.

"—well, you know, it's a different league now. Soft. When I played, you taped it up and got back out there. My kid's sitting out with a sprained knee like it's a broken femur. I didn't raise him to be—"

I close the clip.

My hand is shaking. Water drips from my fingers onto the screen, blurring the progress bar, and I watch the seconds tick on a podcast I'm not going to finish.

Spinner appears at the door, already dressed. "You okay? I shouldn't have sent that."

"What podcast is that?"

"Some sports talk thing. They asked him about your timeline and he just ... went off." Spinner leans against the doorframe. "It's not a big show. Nobody listens."

"Somebody listened enough to send it to you."

He winces. "My agent flagged it. He's got alerts set for the team."

I climb out of the pool and towel off, moving mechanically. My father went on record, publicly, spouting his disapproval of me.

I can already see the headlines. HOUSER SR. QUESTIONS SON'S TOUGHNESS. The comment sections write themselves. People who remember what my father did, people who think the apple doesn't fall far, people who'll use this to paint me as either too soft or too much like him, depending on which narrative gets more clicks.

"Don't read the comments," Spinner says.

"I wasn't going to."

"Sure you weren't." Spinner playfully punches my shoulder, muttering something about his mama, and heads out.

I gather my stuff and drive home, where the condo is dark. Rookie's got a media appearance, and I'm assuming Ella's still at work, so I just sit on the couch like a masochist and listen to the full podcast.

In the twelve-minute interview, my father talks about his own career for most of it—glory days he describes full of hits, playoff runs, and concussions. He makes his suspension sound like a conspiracy to ruin him rather than the right call after a dick move.

"That hit wasn't as bad as they made it," he says, and the host doesn't push back.

Then Dad pivots to me, and the tone shifts to something I recognize from every phone call, every voicemail, every family dinner where he'd watch game tape at the table and point out my mistakes between bites of steak.

"Howie Junior's got talent. Nobody's denying that. But talent without grit is just entertainment. You've got to be willing to sacrifice. I played with a torn rotator cuff in the playoffs. Broken hand. You think I sat out for a sprained knee?"

I lock the phone, setting it face-down on the coffee table. Then I press my palms against my eyes.

The thing about my father is that he's not entirely wrong. To the outside world, it looks exactly like what he's describing, a nepo baby with a famous last name who doesn't have the grit to push through.

And the worst part — the part that sits in my stomach like a stone — is that he'd say it's exactly what he'd expect from me. The party boy. Always chasing the next good time instead of focusing on what matters.

I open the fridge, grab a beer, and crack it on the edge of the counter.

I should call my agent. Why isn't Benny sending me podcast alerts like Spinner's agent? I should issue a statement or do my own interview.

Instead, I drink the beer. And then another. And I'm reaching for a third when Ella walks through the door.

She reads me in three seconds, dropping her bag and kicking off her shoes before crossing the room to interrupt my father's voice in my head.

"What happened?"

"Nothing." I turn away from her, unable to manage my relief at the sight of her compared to my dread of what that means.

"Bernard." She takes the beer from my hand and sets it on the counter. "What happened?"

I show her the podcast. She scans the transcript quickly, jaw tightening, before she closes it.

"He's an asshole."

"He's my father."

"Those things aren't mutually exclusive." She looks at me. Steady. Unafraid. "What do you need?"

I stare at her. I need to hit something. I need to skate until my lungs burn. I need to be someone else's son. I need her to stay right where she is and never move.

"I don't know," I say.

She takes my hand, leads me to the couch, sits beside me, and doesn't talk. She holds my hand, leans her head on my shoulder, and we sit in silence. And it's the best thing I can imagine.

My phone buzzes. I glance over to see a preview of Rookie, in the group chat, sending a clip of his media appearance with three fire emojis. Then Spinner, sending the podcast link to the same chat with the message:

yo Howie you good?

Rookie responds:

wtf is this? Howie your dad is cringe

bro that's fucked up

want me to call him?

I almost laugh. Jason Rujkowski, who cannot remember to buy his sister a game ticket, is offering to call my father and defend me. There's a version of that gesture that's touching. There's another version that's just Rookie — loud, impulsive, charging into situations he doesn't understand because action is faster than thought.

I type back:

I'm good. Don't call him. I'll handle it.

But I don't handle it so much as I sit on the couch with his forbidden sister, whose virginity I exploded. But truly, I think I did something selfish. I could have helped Ella find a nice guy who would be with her in the open. But I wanted her. I wanted her so bad, and damn it, I still want her sitting beside me through all this crap.

When the keys in the lock signal Rookie's arrival, she drops my hand, moves to the chair, and opens the laptop.

Rookie collapses onto the couch beside me, making it feel like Ella is across an ocean. My roommate drops an arm around my shoulder and says, "Dude, your dad is a piece of work. You want to talk about it?"

"Not really."

"Cool. Want to watch game highlights?"

"Sure."

He turns on the TV. Cracks a protein shake. Talks over the play-by-play the way he talks over everything.

I sit there, and I think about Mayhem saying, "tell him" and Ella's hand that I can't hold, and my father calling me soft on a podcast, and the bomb I'm building that gets bigger every day.

I should tell Rookie tonight. Right now, while we're all here. *"Hey, man, I need to tell you something about me and your sister."*

The words are right there.

Instead, I say, "Nice pass," and Rookie nods, and the moment dies. The woman I love says nothing, eventually closing the laptop and wandering off to my bed alone while her brother—my best friend—has no idea that everything he thinks he knows about his life is wrong.

I WASN'T REALLY EXPECTING TO SLEEP BEFORE MY BOARDS. I TRIED studying all night, but my thoughts kept drifting to Bernard and his struggle with his dad's shitty attitude.

I had a brief revelation that his father's behavior sounds similar to CTE case studies I've read, but that seems like a conversation above my pay grade. Which is really low.

I drag myself out of bed before dawn on Leap Day, shower, and toss on a sweatsuit I'd never wear in public. But a life-determining test doesn't count as public.

I tiptoe out of the bedroom expecting a dark living room and sleeping sex tutor, but instead I find the stove light on and Bernard awake, dressed, standing at the counter with two steaming mugs of coffee.

"Morning," he says, sliding a mug toward me.

I know that today is his day to sleep in, that he and my brother have game film and a light workout, but no other team responsibilities. So why is Bernard Houser up hours before he needs to be? "You didn't have to get up."

"I know."

I wrap my hands around the mug and let the heat seep into my fingers. Jason's door is closed. The apartment is silent except for the refrigerator and the faint sounds of the building elevator.

Bernard leans against the counter across from me. "I figure, I must be a pretty good tutor since you aced the sex stuff."

My jaw drops, and I smack his arm. "Quiet. What are you trying to do?"

He rolls his eyes. "I just meant, I knew you'd be nervous about your test, and I wanted to tell you what I do before games. Prep tutoring."

My heart rate slows infinitesimally. "If it involves a special jockstrap, I don't want to know."

He smiles, the warmth of his energy soothing me. "I close my eyes, and I picture the ice. Not the game — just the ice. The feel of it under my skates. The cold air. The sound of a clean pass hitting tape." He taps the counter. "I don't think about winning or losing. I just put myself in a place where I know what I'm doing. Where my body takes over, and my brain gets out of the way."

I stare at him. My body certainly excels when *he* is what I'm doing. But my brain has never cooperated that way. Ever.

Bernard leans closer, though. "You know what you're doing, Ella. Your body knows this stuff. Just let it take over."

My eyes sting. I blink it away and take a sip of coffee that burns my tongue. "That's actually good advice."

"I have my moments."

My phone buzzes on the counter. Then again. Then three times in rapid succession.

MCKENZIE

YOU'VE GOT THIS, QUEEN 👑 Remember: the answer is always assess before you intervene

AARTHI

Ella Rujkowski, you are smarter than any test.
I believe in you. Also, my mother wants to
know if you're single. Ignore that part.

MCKENZIE

Wait, Aarthi's mom wants to set Ella up??

AARTHI

IGNORE THAT PART

Then a message rolls in from a number I saved last week:

JULES

Good luck today, Ella! You're stronger than
you think. See you Saturday

I press the phone against my chest. I have people who believe in me and know what today means. My own parents have barely reached out since I moved in with Jason. To be fair, they don't call him much either.

It's too scary to trust their faith in me, though. It's like this thing with Bernard...it tastes sweet, but feels fleeting. All dependent on me actually passing a test that really seems impossible.

Bernard walks around the counter and begins to rinse his mug, opening the dishwasher, wrinkling his nose adorably at the odor that wafts out. "When do you need to be there, Ella? I'll drop you off."

I set my own mug down. "Bernard."

"Yeah?"

"I think I should take the bus to the testing center."

Something shifts in his face. "Let me drive you."

"It's better if you keep your distance today. Jason could wake up, and—"

"Ella."

"I need to do this on my own." I press both palms to the

ostentatious marble countertop. "And honestly ...after my boards, I'll be out of both your hair."

He goes still. "What do you mean?"

"If by some miracle I pass, I'll have a real paycheck. I can find my own apartment. Get out of your room. Give you back your bed and your closet and your drawer." I try to smile. "And if I fail — which, let's be realistic — I'll head back to Minnesota to my parents' house and figure out next steps."

He stares at me like I just told him I'm moving to Mars.

"Either way," I say, "it's time for me to stop crashing with my brother."

He grips the edge of the counter and frowns. I watch him choose his words the way he does when something matters — carefully, slowly, fighting his own instinct just to say the first thing that comes to mind.

"Okay," he says.

That's all. But his jaw is tight, and his hand on the counter has gone white at the knuckles, and I know that okay is not what he wanted to say.

I finish my coffee and start gathering my things, putting on my coat and pink sneakers. I smile, remembering I had them on at the airport when Bernard picked me up. But I shouldn't smile about Bernard. Not in that way.

Instead, I remind myself of his visualization advice, give him a wave, and walk toward the door.

The bus to the testing center takes forty minutes. I sit by the window, close my eyes, and picture the ER. The feel of a blood bag in my hands. The steady beep of a monitor. The calm that settles over me when a patient needs me, and my body knows what to do.

I don't think about passing or failing. I just put myself in a place where I know what I'm doing.

———

The testing center is a beige building in a strip mall between a sub shop and a dry cleaner. Inside, it smells like carpet cleaner and anxiety. I check in, lock my phone and bag in a cubby, and sit down at a computer terminal in a room full of strangers who all look as terrified as I feel.

The first question appears on the screen. A patient presents with acute chest pain radiating to the left arm. Which intervention should the nurse perform first?

I read it twice. The words try to swim, but I hold them in place, hear Bernard's voice asking the question out loud in my head, and click my answer.

The next question loads. And the next. And the next.

Some I know instantly — the trauma questions, the emergency protocols, the things I do with my hands every shift. Some I wrestle with — pharmacology dosages, lab values, and priority-setting questions where every answer seems half-right. I read each one twice. I breathe. I let my body take over.

The computer shuts off at question 88.

I stare at the blank screen. The minimum is 75. The maximum is 145. I have no idea if 88 is good or catastrophic. The screen tells me results will be available in 48 hours and thanks me for completing the examination.

And ... that's it.

I have now completed the thing that's been standing in my way. There's nothing more to do but grab my stuff and head outside into the February chill.

The sky is gray and flat, and the air bites my cheeks as I cross the sidewalk, not knowing if I'm a nurse.

I start walking toward the bus stop, legs hollow and brain full of static.

But then I see the G-Wagon.

Parked outside the sub shop is a familiar black SUV, with a familiar, enormous man leaning against the rear bumper. He has his arms crossed over his massive chest, a hat pulled low over his curls. He looks like an ad for something expensive and irresponsible.

The sob hits me before I can stop it — not sadness, not failure, just the raw, cracking overwhelm of someone showing up when you told them not to because they knew you needed them to.

My vision blurs and my throat seizes, and I'm walking, and then I'm running across the parking lot, backpack bouncing against my spine, and I crash into him so hard he rocks back against the bumper.

His arms close around me, tight and solid, wrapping me up the way they did that night he climbed into bed beside me by accident. Except this time he's holding me on purpose, in broad daylight.

"I've got you," he says against my hair.

I press my face into his chest and cry. It's like he released a blood pressure cuff for my emotions.

His big hand strokes my hair. His lips press against the top of my head. He just holds me and lets me shake and breathes steadily against my hair like he's trying to lend me his calm.

"You came," I manage.

"Of course I did."

"I told you not to."

"You tell me a lot of things I ignore." His cheek settles against the top of my head. "It's part of my charm."

I laugh into his hoodie. It comes out wet and broken, but it's a laugh, and his arms tighten, and for thirty seconds the world is just this: Bernard's chest against my face, Bernard's hand in my hair, Bernard's lips on my head, and the feeling of warm support.

Then I hear a car.

Bass music thuds loud enough that I glance over to see an expensive car driving too fast, screeching to a halt in the lot. I recognize Jason's souped-up SUV, which comes to a halt a foot away from Bernard and me.

Through the windshield, I see my brother's face, frozen, like he's watching a replay of a penalty the ref missed.

I see my brother notice Bernard's arms around me. Bernard's hand in my hair. And my tear-streaked face pressed against his best friend's chest.

Jason kills the engine. The silence is thunderous.

He opens the door, steps out, and stands in the cold with his jaw locked and his eyes moving between me and Bernard while he finally sees what I've been trying to pretend wasn't happening.

My brother growls and finally says, "What the fuck is this?"

JASON'S FACE TELLS ME EVERYTHING BEFORE HIS MOUTH OPENS.

He stands beside his SUV with the door hanging open, and I watch the calculation happen in real time. My arms around his sister, my hand in her hair, her face pressed against my chest. Not a drunk kiss at Gianna's. Not something he can file under "Howie being Howie."

This is what it looks like when two people are together.

"What the fuck is this?" he says.

Ella pulls back from my chest, but I keep one arm around her shoulder. Instinct. Protective. Which is the wrong move because now I'm standing between her and her brother like a wall, and Jason's eyes track the gesture, and his jaw goes tight enough to crack a mouthguard.

"Jason," Ella starts. "Let me—"

"I'm asking him." Jason points at me. His hand shakes. "I'm asking you, Howie. What the fuck is this?"

My brain runs through a dozen responses. Lies, deflections, jokes. The Howie playbook is full of exit strategies for uncomfortable situations. I could tell him it's nothing. I could tell him she was upset about her boards, and I was just comforting her.

Instead, I say, "This is exactly what you think it is."

His face goes dark. "Excuse me?" He steps forward. "You're fucking my sister?"

"I'm with your sister. There's a difference." Ella gasps, a tiny sound I can't analyze right now.

"The hell you are," Jason shouts, stepping closer, leaning back. I know the look of Rookie gearing up for a fight, and I'm not about to let that happen within arm's reach of the woman I love.

A low sound rumbles from Rookie's throat. "Since when?"

I don't answer fast enough. Ella says, "Since — it's been—"

"Since when, Howie?"

"Weeks," I say, because he deserves the truth even if it kills us.

The sound Jason makes isn't a word. It's something from the back of his throat, raw and animal, and I see his fists clench at his sides, and I know what's coming because I've seen Jason Rujkowski throw a punch a hundred times. On the ice, in the locker room, once in a bar in Minnesota, when a guy grabbed a waitress. He's fast, he's mean, and he doesn't miss.

"I told you to stay away from her." His voice is low now, which is worse than the yelling. Jason quiet is Jason dangerous. "I told you, man. One rule that mattered. One fucking rule."

"You actually have three rules, Rookie, and they're all immature." I try to move Ella further away, out of Rookie's wingspan, but she's rooted in place under my arm.

Her brother's face goes dark. "Excuse me?"

I mock his voice, not caring what this does to his temper. "Don't wear your gear. Don't eat your food. Don't touch your sister. Those are the rules of a twelve-year-old, Jason. We're not kids anymore."

"You mother fucker." He steps forward and shoves me with both hands, hard enough to knock me back against the bumper. Ella grabs Jason's arm, and he shakes her off.

"Don't touch me right now, Ellie."

"Jason, stop—"

"Did you plan this?" He's in my face now, close enough for me to see the vein in his temple, the redness in his eyes. "Is that why you told me about this stupid test? You wanted me to come up here and see you?"

"I told you to text her, asshole. Like maybe ask her how things are going." I have both my feet under me again, my shoulders tense, ready to trade blows.

Behind me, I hear Ella grumbling. "Jason," she says, and her voice is steady now, the trauma nurse voice, the de-escalation voice. "Bernard has been good to me. This isn't—"

"Good to you? He's been lying to me for weeks. You've BOTH been lying to me."

"Because you would have reacted exactly like this!"

"BECAUSE HE'S MY BEST FRIEND!" Jason has both hands in his hair now, which at least means he's not about to hit me with them. "What the fuck do I do when he fucks you over, Ella? Stop speaking to my best friend?"

To my surprise, Ella steps up in his face and snarls at him. "I never asked you to defend me. And I never had a chance to show you I'm perfectly capable of fighting my own relationship battles because YOU SCARED ALL MEN AWAY FROM ME WITH YOUR STUPID RULES."

The parking lot rings with Rujkowski anger. A woman coming out of the sub shop freezes, sandwich in hand, and hurries to her car. Jason is breathing hard. Ella is breathing hard. I'm standing between them with my back against the G-Wagon and my knee throbbing and the full weight of Mayhem's warning sitting on my chest.

The bomb went off.

Jason turns back to me. Something shifts in his face. Past the hurt, past the betrayal, into something colder. "You know what? I should have seen it coming when she came to stay with us. You're just like your old man."

The words are a blade to an artery, but Rookie's not done yet.

"He couldn't keep his hands to himself either," Jason says. "Had to take what he wanted, consequences be damned. Didn't matter who got hurt."

I feel the blood leave my face. My hands drop to my sides. Of all the things Jason could say — and he could say a lot; he knows me better than almost anyone alive — he picked the one thing that goes straight through the bone.

"That's not…" My voice sounds wrong. Thin. "That's not what this is."

"No? Because from where I'm standing, it looks like my best friend took advantage of my little sister while she was living under my roof with nowhere else to go."

"He didn't take advantage of me." Ella steps between us, her cheeks are red, her eyes bright and furious. "I started this. I'm a grown woman, and I made a choice." I can't help but notice what she's not saying in my defense. She's not yelling that she loves me, that she wants to be with me for real.

But I can't focus on the absent words because Jason's not done yet. "Some choice," he snarls.

"Stop it."

"You've been here two months, Ella. And you're already…"

"Already what?" Her voice is sharp and mean as his. "Already making a mess? Already screwing things up? Is that what you were going to say?"

Jason hesitates.

"Because that's what you think, right? That's what everyone thinks. Ella can't pass a test, Ella can't hold a job, and Ella can't make smart decisions. Little Baby Rookie, always messing things up."

"I didn't say that."

"You were going to." She steps closer to her brother. I see something in her face I haven't seen before, not the calm nurse, not the dry wit, but real, undiluted fury. "I have been a spectator in YOUR life since I was in diapers. Every car ride, every tournament, every family dinner that was actually a scouting report. And the one time — the ONE time — I start making my own choices, building my own life, you can't handle it because you don't know how to communicate boundaries with your friend."

Jason stares at her. I stare at her.

"I really hoped," she says, and her voice drops, the anger giving way to something rawer, "that once I started doing things for myself, you'd actually show up for me. That you'd be a better brother than the one I grew up with."

"I DID show up!" He gestures at his car, at the parking lot, at the whole scene. "I'm literally here, Ella! I drove across the city to pick you up from your test because Howie told me it was important!"

"Right. You're here because BERNARD told you I had something important. When else have you shown up? Not the airport. Not in the dark when it's snowing, and I need to get home from work. You're too much of a selfish dick."

Ella's nose is red, and I think briefly about how adorable she looks before I remember that she's in the middle of a fight with her brother... my best friend. She takes a fortifying breath and lets loose. "You know who shows up for me every day? Your best friend. So yeah. I'm sleeping with him. A lot. Huge fuckfest right under your nose."

The sentence hangs in the cold air. Jason's fists unclench and clench again. Then he steps forward, fast, and his right hand connects with my face.

The punch is clean and hard, sending my head snapping to the side. I taste copper. My knee buckles, and I grab the bumper to keep from going down. The pain is bright and immediate, but nothing's broken. I've taken worse on the ice from guys who meant it more.

This was the punch of a man who wants to hurt his best

friend just enough to feel like he did something about the hurt in his own chest.

"Bernard!" Ella is between us instantly, hands on my face, tilting my jaw toward the light. Nurse mode. Assessing. Her fingers probe the bones around my eye, checking alignment, watching my pupils. "Look at me. Follow my finger."

"I'm fine."

"You're bleeding."

"I'm *fine*, Ella."

She spins on Jason. "Are you done?"

He's standing three feet away, cradling his right hand — he punched wrong, probably strained something in his fingers, and the irony of a professional athlete hurting himself throwing a punch in a strip mall parking lot would be funny if everything weren't falling apart.

"Yeah," Jason says. His voice is hollow. "We're done."

He turns, walks to his SUV, and gets in. The door slams. The engine roars. The bass kicks back in, absurdly loud for the weight of the moment, and Jason Rujkowski peels out of the parking lot, tires screeching.

Ella and I stand in the cold silence afterward. Her hands are still on my face. My cheek throbs. A thin line of blood runs down my face, and she wipes it with her thumb, so gently.

"Let me see," she murmurs, turning my head. "It's superficial. You'll bruise."

"Ella."

"You should ice it when you get home. Twenty minutes on, twenty off." She steps back. Drops her hands. Wraps her arms around herself. "I need to figure some things out."

"Come home with me. We can talk—"

"I need space, Bernard." She looks at the sub shop. "I'm going to go sit in there for a while. Maybe get something to eat. Think."

"Ella, your brother—"

"Please." Her voice is quiet. "Go home."

I don't want to leave her in a strip mall parking lot. Every cell in my body revolts at the idea of getting in my car and driving away from Ella Rujkowski, standing in the cold with my blood on her thumb.

But she asked. And I've spent weeks learning that Ella asks for very little and means it completely when she does.

"Okay," I say. "I'll go."

She nods. Turns toward the sub shop. Pauses. "Ice your jaw. And your knee. Don't skip the knee just because your face hurts more acutely."

"Yes, ma'am."

She almost smiles. Then she walks inside, and the glass door swings shut behind her, and I'm alone in the parking lot with a busted friendship and the wreckage of every secret I kept too long.

Because I am incapable of being a real adult, I have nowhere to sleep tonight that won't get me murdered. I pull out my phone and text Mayhem.

> Can I crash at your place tonight?

He responds in four seconds.

> Door's open.

And so I don't drive back to the condo to face Rookie, or stare at the evidence of Ella in my room. I pull out of the lot and head toward Observatory Hill to crash on yet another teammate's couch.

CHAPTER 21
ELLA

The sub shop is warm and smells like bread and pickles, and the fluorescent lights buzz overhead at a frequency that matches the static in my brain. A teenager behind the counter watches me sit alone in a booth for forty minutes and probably wonders if I'm having a breakdown.

I probably am.

I'm definitely running through scenarios while staring off into space, calculating life options.

If I failed the NCLEX, my provisional hire at Mercy is done-zo. No job. No paycheck. No apartment fund. No reason to stay in Pittsburgh.

If I passed, I have a career. But I also have a brother who won't speak to me and a man I can't be with and a life that just detonated in a parking lot outside this very establishment.

I eat the pickle, toss the sandwich, and leave the sub shop. I hop on the bus back to my brother's condo, leaning my head against the cold window and watching Pittsburgh slide past in the growing dusk.

The place is dark when I let myself in. Jason's door is closed. Music thumps behind it — not the victory playlist he blasts after wins. Something heavier. Angrier. He's not coming out any time soon.

The couch is empty. Bernard's blanket is folded neatly on the arm. His pillow is stacked on top. The living room looks the way it did before I moved in, before he started sleeping here so I could have his bed.

I check my phone, and there's nothing. Nothing from Bernard. Nothing from Jason. The last text in my inbox is from McKenzie, three hours ago, wondering how the test went.

I can't answer that. I don't know how the test went. I don't know how anything went.

I slide into Bernard's bed, and my mind spins. My body heats and cools at the memory of the test shutting off after 88 questions, of my relief at seeing Bernard in the parking lot after, of my anguish when Jason found out what's been going on.

Honestly, it was well past time to put words to what's been going on with Bernard Houser. What started as a check-list item for me, a need to enter a relationship with experience, the way my externship was meant to prepare me for a real nursing job ... shifted into something I never imagined.

Every stolen moment with Bernard felt sparkly, soothing, exhilarating. Way more satisfying than sliding into instinct mode with a trauma victim. Bernard might just be my person.

Except that's gone to shit.

———

I sleep fitfully, well past my usual wake-up time. I can tell the apartment is empty. Jason must have gone to practice, or else just left me here to wallow in misery.

My phone rings, but I let it go to voicemail because I can't produce human speech right now. I do hoist myself out of bed and splash water on my face, chugging some liquid right from the faucet before dabbing myself dry on a towel that smells like Bernard's body wash.

A voicemail notification pops up on my phone, and I press play on the message, letting it echo off the bathroom tile.

"Ella, it's Susan. I need you to come in tomorrow morning before your shift. There's a meeting with me and the nurse manager about your position. It's important." A pause. "Call me back when you get this."

She hangs up. No "honey." No warmth. Just a summons.

I set the phone down and stare at myself in the mirror.

The nurse manager doesn't meet with externs to debrief on boards. No, this vague meeting summons is about next steps. And Susan's tone on that voicemail didn't sound like someone delivering good news.

I failed.

The certainty settles into my body like the chilled water in Jason's tap. I failed the NCLEX, and the hospital knows, and tomorrow they're going to sit me down and tell me my provisional hire is over, and I need to move on.

I walk back out into a bedroom that smells like both of us, that has my clothes in the closet and my shoes on the floor and his body wash in the bathroom and the ghost of every night we spent tangled together in those sheets.

Not for long. I know I can't face Susan, can't sit there and keep my composure while they tell me everything I worked for was wasted.

I pull my suitcase out from under the bed and re-pack it methodically.

The drawer Bernard cleared for me empties in minutes. The closet hangers swing bare, and the space Bernard made looks exactly the way it did the day he opened it — empty, waiting for someone who might stay.

I set the suitcase by the door and sit on the edge of the bed.

I should call Aarthi and McKenzie. I'd want to know if

they were leaving. But I honestly can't handle my emotions to listen to their words right now, either, so I chicken out and send them a text instead.

> Heading home for a while. Things got complicated.

McKenzie responds in seconds:

> What?? Are you ok??

> AARTHI

> What happened? Do you need us to come over?

> ME

> I'm ok. Just some family stuff. I'll explain later.

I lock the phone before they can respond and look around the room. The bed is made because I make it every morning, a habit from childhood when my room had to be presentable for Jason's teammates who'd come over after practice and dump their coats on my bed. A bed I'm about to sleep in again, tail between my legs. Every bit the failure my family always thought I was.

At least I'm not a virgin anymore.

In the living room, I grab Jason's laptop from the counter and navigate to an airline site, where I find decent one-way airfare from Pittsburgh to Minneapolis.

I stare at the booking page. The cursor blinks in the payment field. There's enough in my account to either pay my student loan bill or buy this ticket, and I'm honestly not sure which is the least responsible option.

I have got to get out of my head, find some clarity. Figure shit out.

An idea slides into place, and I know where I need to go to

get one last whiff of power before I fly off to face my shitty music. Towing my suitcase behind me, I grab a bus and head for the silks studio.

It's open hours this morning, and there are just a few women practicing inversions when I arrive a half hour later. I wedge my bag against the shoe cubbies, kick off my Chucks, and find a length of purple fabric.

I grip the material and my palms sting, my arms burn. But I find the foot lock and hold it, suspended, three feet off the ground, then four. I lean back, extend my free leg, and arch my neck the way Jules taught me, and I feel my body do a thing it knows how to do — hold itself up.

I climb higher. My muscles shake, but they hold. The fabric bites my hands, and my foot aches, but I don't come down. I hang there in the purple silk in an almost-empty studio, and I feel the weight of this entire week pressing on me from every direction — the test, the voicemail, the parking lot, Bernard's blood on my thumb, Jason's face, the suitcase.

I don't cry. I just hold on.

My body knows things my brain hasn't caught up to yet. My body knows how to grip when everything is slipping. My body knows how to stay suspended when there's nothing solid underneath.

I might lose my job. I might fly home. Tomorrow, everything I built here might crumble.

But right now I'm in the air, and the fabric is holding, and I'm not falling yet.

CHAPTER 22
HOWIE

MAYHEM'S COUCH IS WORSE THAN ROOKIE'S, BUT IT SEEMS LIKE IT costs less, at least.

It's a brown corduroy thing that smells like dog, even though Mayhem is a cat dad, and my feet hang off the end. His Observatory Hill house is quiet — no barge horns, drunk people sauntering around outside, just birds and the distant hum of Riverview Park waking up.

My cheek throbs. My knee throbs. My everything throbs.

I lie here staring at Mayhem's ceiling, which has cracks in the plaster like a regular-person house, and I think about Ella telling me to go home.

So I went. Because she asked. Because I'm trying to be the man who listens, not the man who takes.

I thought Mayhem would talk to me for once, tell me what to do about that apartment with her clothes in my closet and the ghosts of my promises filling the space.

But he just fed me along with his furball and went to bed.

Mayhem appears in the doorway now, though, with two mugs of coffee. He's already dressed in black sweats, bare feet. He is fully awake, like he's been up for hours reading. He hands me a mug and sits in the armchair across from me and doesn't speak.

We drink our coffee in silence for a few minutes. I fully understand why Cappy nicknamed this guy Mayhem. He's anything but. Dude is stoic and calm, but clearly filled with opinions he's patiently waiting for you to acknowledge.

"What's the plan?" he asks eventually.

"I don't have one."

He nods. Sips. Waits. His orange cat wanders into the room and sits beside Mayhem so both of them are staring at me, waiting.

"I don't know what to do, Cameron." I almost never use his real name. It comes out raw. "She told me to leave, and it felt like abandoning her in a parking lot. But I also don't think it would have been right to insist on putting her in my car against her—"

My phone rings with Rookie's custom sound effect: the "where's the beef" commercial from the 1900's.

My stomach drops. I stare at it until Mayhem says, "Answer it."

So I do.

"Howie." Jason's voice is wrong. Not angry. Not the low, dangerous quiet from the parking lot. This is something tight, fast, like Rookie is barely holding it together. "Is Ella with you?"

"No. Why?"

"She's gone."

I sit up so fast that coffee sloshes on the corduroy. "What do you mean she's gone?"

"I mean, she's GONE, dude. Her stuff — the closet is empty. Everything she had is gone." His breath is ragged. "She left my laptop open on an airline site about flights to Minneapolis."

The floor tilts. I grip the arm of the couch.

"I tried calling her," Rookie says. "Straight to voicemail. I texted. Nothing. She's not at the hospital. I already called the ER desk."

"Rookie—"

"I chased her away." His voice cracks, and I hear something I've almost never heard from Jason Rujkowski — not anger, not bravado, but genuine, chest-deep anguish. "I drove her out of my home. My own sister. She came to Pittsburgh because I told her I'd help her out, and I sucked at that, and now she's going back to Minnesota."

I close my eyes. My own guilt is a living thing in my chest, clawing for space next to the fear.

"We both did this," I say. "I should have told you weeks ago. I should have been honest with you instead of sneaking around behind your back. That's on me."

Rookie is quiet for a beat. "Yeah. It is." Another beat. "But I'm the one who punched you and told her she was making a mess of things. After her big exam." His voice drops. "What kind of brother does that?"

"The kind who shows up to drive her home from a test he didn't even know about until yesterday."

"And then ruins it."

"Yeah," I say. "And then ruins it. Like I said, we both contributed to this mess."

Mayhem is already on his feet, pulling on shoes. He heard enough from my side of the conversation. I put Rookie on speaker.

"Rookie, I'm at Mayhem's. I'm going to find her."

"How? She's not answering—"

"Call the crew, and we split up," I offer, and Mayhem nods. I grab my keys from the coffee table and shove my feet into my shoes. "You should check the airport. Spinner has McKenzie's number."

"Who?" Rookie sounds like he, too, is grabbing keys.

I pinch the bridge of my nose, frustrated that this guy missed so much in the short time Ella was living with us.

"One of Ella's nurse friends. They might have heard from her."

"Okay. Yeah. Okay." Rookie's voice steadies. "Howie."

"Yeah?"

"Find her. Please."

I hang up. Mayhem is already at the door, phone in hand, texting Spinner. "Go," he says. "I'll coordinate."

I drive, swinging by the hospital, not sure why. It's not like I can go in there and ask if she showed up to work.

But as I'm swinging through uptown, a thought occurs to me. Ella was looking up airfare, but she's also been working on her own version of flight.

As I drive to the silk studio, running yellow lights, muscles straining, I know that my hunch is correct. I just know Ella will be in here, trying to soar.

Because I know Ella Rujkowski the way I know the ice, it's pure instinct understanding at this point. When everything falls apart, Ella runs to the thing that makes her feel strong. The thing that's hers.

I park crooked in front of the studio and half-jog to the entrance. Through the glass I can see the silks hanging from the ceiling, purple and red, and one of them is taut.

I push through the door.

She's in the air like a gorgeous bird. She looks so strong and powerful, back arched, thick leg sticking out behind her. The swell of her belly glows in the sun streaming through the studio window. I've never seen anything more beautiful.

Her suitcase sits against the wall by the shoe cubbies, packed and waiting for her to come down, wheel it to the airport, and disappear from my life.

"The only flying you should be doing," I say, and my voice echoes in the studio, "is down from there and into my arms."

Her head snaps toward me. She wobbles on the silk and tightens her grip, staring down at me from her perch. This beautiful, stubborn, brilliant woman who saves lives and climbs fabric and makes me feel like I'm special.

My black eye must look spectacular because her expression shifts from shock to concern to something softer. "Bernard. Your face."

"It's fine. Get down here."

She descends a little awkwardly and lands on the mat. "You found me," she says.

"Of course, I found you." I step closer. "I'm a St. Bernard, remember? Search and rescue. It's what I do."

Her face crumples — not into tears, into something between a laugh and a sob. "You enormous, ridiculous man."

"Come here, Ella."

She crosses the mat and walks into my arms, and I hold her the way I've been wanting to since I caught sight of her at the airport — completely, with everything I have, like she's the thing I've been looking for without knowing I was lost.

Then I kiss her. Not a stolen kitchen kiss or something secret. I kiss her like she ought to be kissed, in the daylight, openly.

When we break for air, I tuck her head against my chest and tell her, "You scared me. And your brother. What made you leave?"

She pulls back and looks up at me. "I got a voicemail from Susan." Her lip wobbles. "She wants me to come in for a meeting. About my position." Her jaw tightens. "I think I failed, Bernard."

"You don't know that."

"The tone of her voice—"

"You don't know." I hold her face in both hands. "Ella. You are the most capable person I have ever met. You aced every practice test for weeks. You are a goddamn incredible nurse, and you are going to walk into that meeting tomorrow and hear what Susan has to say."

"I'm scared."

"I know. But you can be scared. I've watched you do scared. You do scared better than anyone." I press my forehead against hers. "I'll drive you there. I'll sit in the parking lot and wait. Whatever you need, but just stay. Please."

She blinks up at me with tears near her lashes and swallows, nodding almost imperceptibly. But I'll take it.

I release her and walk to the wall where her suitcase sits propped against the cubbies. I grab the handle and roll it toward the door.

"What are you doing?" she asks.

"Putting this in my car and taking you home."

"Bernard—"

"Your place is in Pittsburgh, Ella." I turn to look at her. "Your friends are here. Your job is here. Your weird circus hobby is here."

"It's not weird."

"Your glorious hobby is here." I hold out my hand. "And I'm here. So let's go home."

She stares at my hand. Then at me. I lean forward until our fingers touch, and then I wrap her hand in mine for good.

We walk out of the studio into the cold March morning. I toss her suitcase in the back of the G-Wagon beside my gym bag and open her door. She climbs in, and the heated seat hums to life. She makes that sound, the tiny sigh, a pleased little groan I've been obsessed with since January.

I pull away from the curb with our fingers threaded together, the way they've been in the dark. But that was before. Now that I have her with me in broad daylight, I'm not letting go.

CHAPTER 23
ELLA

BERNARD DRIVES ME STRAIGHT TO MERCY HOSPITAL AFTER I confirm with Susan that I can come in now rather than before a shift.

He holds my hand, rubs my leg as I breathe through my anxiety. I can hoist myself into the air. I can sit across from someone and listen while they let me know my fate. I can do this.

I keep glancing at Bernard. His black eye deepened into a purple crescent, and I wonder briefly if he chipped an orbital bone again.

"Stop assessing me," he says.

"You should get that checked out."

"I had other priorities last night." He squeezes my hand. "I'll see the trainer tomorrow, okay?"

I nod and try the visualization exercises Bernard told me about before my boards. I imagine Susan telling me she's proud of me, that I get to stay.

By the time Bernard pulls into the parking garage, I'm almost calm.

I unclip my seatbelt and sit there for a second, staring at the concrete wall. "Am I too sweaty and casual to talk to my boss about this?"

He cracks a crooked smile and shakes his head. "Would you feel more comfortable in bloody scrubs?"

I huff. "Honestly, maybe."

Bernard cups my cheek and turns me to face him, his beautiful eyes warm and encouraging. "Whatever happens in there," he says, "know that you're amazing. A piece of paper doesn't define you or your ability."

"I know."

"Do you?"

I look at him. "Yeah," I say. "I think I do."

I get out, cross the lot, and summon the elevator up to the admin offices. The hallway smells like floor wax and printer toner, a different universe from the ER's antiseptic chaos. My sneakers squeak on the tile.

Susan is waiting outside the nurse manager's office. She's in her usual scrubs, reading glasses pushed up on her head, and when she sees me, she smiles. She doesn't seem upset and doesn't appear to judge my outfit.

"There she is," Susan says, draping an arm around my shoulder. "Come on in."

I want to let myself feel relief, but the voice in my head whispers that Susan could be preparing to let me down with love.

The nurse manager's name is Monique. She's a Black woman in her mid-fifties with gray hair and reading glasses on a chain, the kind of woman who has framed diplomas on every wall and a candy dish on her desk that nobody touches because it feels like a trap.

I sit in the chair across from her, fold my hands in my lap, and brace for the word "unfortunately."

Monique opens a folder. "Ella, your NCLEX results came back."

I stop breathing.

"You nailed it, my dear."

The room goes very still. Susan puts a hand on my shoulder. Monique nods, smiling. "You made our externship program look very good indeed. In a time where we really needed a win." She opens a folder and gestures at the paperwork. "Combined with your clinical evaluations and the feedback from the ER attendings, you are quite the candidate for a permanent nursing position."

I open my mouth, and nothing comes out.

"We have some options for you." Monique slides a printout across the desk. "There's an opening on the med-surg unit. Day shift, excellent mentorship. It's a competitive placement, and frankly, it's unusual to offer it to a new grad."

I look at the printout. Steady hours. Normal schedule. Patients who are stable.

"Or," Susan says, leaning against the doorframe with her arms crossed, "you stay with me in the ER."

I look at Susan, who raises an eyebrow. I think about the kid with internal bleeding. The quarter swallower. The panic attack woman I sat with and made laugh. The sound of the trauma bay when everything is moving fast, and my hands are steady, and my mind is clear.

"ER," I say.

Susan grins. "That's my girl."

Monique makes a note in the folder and smiles again. "An excellent choice. Congratulations, Ella. Please remember to negotiate with me regarding this signing bonus."

She slides a piece of paper across the desk and looks at me expectantly.

Susan chuckles behind me, coughing the word "double" into her fist.

I glance at the number, a big one, and laugh uncomfortably. "Um, I guess ...I was expecting double that number."

Monique purses her lips, and I cannot tell what she is thinking. Did I just cost myself the job? I am so unprepared for this. But Monique taps the desk. "We are prepared to offer fifty percent more."

A puff of air escapes my mouth, which is good because it masks the scream I'm trying to stifle. I will have actual money now to get my own place to live, a paycheck to chip away at my student loans.

"Thank you." My voice sounds strange to me. Thick. "Thank you both."

Monique has already moved on to other work, typing furiously as she nods. Susan takes my arm and guides me into the hallway, where she gives me a squeeze. "I knew it, honey. You're a natural."

My body swirls with emotions I can't name. Relief? Excitement? Could this be what pride feels like? I feel an overwhelming pull to call Bernard.

But I meet Susan's gaze and admit to her, "You scared me with that voicemail."

"I scared you?" She laughs. "I was trying to be professional. Believe me, I wanted to call you screaming."

I laugh, and it shakes loose something that's been lodged in my windpipe since yesterday. Maybe longer.

"One more thing," Susan says, adjusting her glasses. "Now that you're permanent staff, I expect you to get me into a Fury game. Your brother gets good seats, right?"

"I'll see what I can do."

She pats my back and heads toward the elevator. I stand in the hallway for a minute. The fluorescent lights buzz. A janitor pushes a mop cart past me. Somewhere below, the ER is humming along without me, handling whatever Pittsburgh throws at it, and tomorrow I'll be down there as a real RN.

I take the skybridge back to the garage. Bernard's G-Wagon sits right where I left it, heat shimmering from the engine in the cold air. I open the door and climb in.

He turns to me, face steady in anticipation.

"I passed."

His eyes brighten. "Of course you did."

"They offered me a permanent job and…a bonus."

"Ella." He reaches across the console and cups the back of my neck and pulls me toward him and kisses my forehead, my cheek, my mouth. "Of course they did."

"You don't seem surprised."

"I'm not." He releases me, turns on the engine, puts the car in gear, and pulls out of the spot. "I was so sure of it that I already called your friends. Aarthi and McKenzie are meeting us at Gianna's."

"You called my friends?"

He nods, glancing over his shoulder to turn onto Fifth Avenue. "Spinner had McKenzie's number. Everyone's been worried about you since your brother saw you were looking at flights."

My stomach tightens. "Jason?"

"He's been scouring the airport looking for you since this morning, Ella. He thought you flew home." Bernard glances at me. "He wants to be there for you."

I lean back in the heated seat and close my eyes. The sun is out. The car is warm. Bernard is beside me, and my friends are waiting, and my brother is coming, and I just became a real nurse.

The air around me feels different now. My body is ... not relieved, exactly. Not happy necessarily. I feel a little like a joint that's been out of alignment for twenty-three years just clicked into place, and the pain I thought was permanent turns out to have been transient.

I did something difficult. I did it well. And the people around me--the ones I found, the ones I chose--chose me back. I trust that. They want to celebrate. Not because I'm somebody's sister or somebody's afterthought, but because I'm Ella, and Ella is enough.

I open my eyes and look at Bernard's profile. This man helped make all this happen for me. He gained nothing from this. Except, I guess, my heart.

"Bernard."

"Yeah?"
"Thank you."
He takes my hand. "For what?"
"Everything."
He lifts my hand to his mouth and kisses my knuckles.

CHAPTER 24
HOWIE

CHAPTER 24
HOWIE

GIANNA MEETS US AT THE DOOR WITH A WOODEN SPOON AND A grin. "I heard there's a new nurse in the 'burgh."

Ella blushes and nods, and Gianna pulls her in for a hug.

"McKenzie's been here for twenty minutes telling everyone how awesome you are." Gianna ushers us into the back room. "I made something special. Sit."

The meatball joint is full. McKenzie spots Ella and screams — a full, fangirl whoop that makes Spinner flinch, and Mayhem raise an eyebrow — and launches herself across the room to grab Ella in a hug that lifts her off the ground. Aarthi is right behind, calmer but bright-eyed, squeezing Ella's arm and saying something I can't hear over McKenzie's continued shrieking.

The PAWs are out in force, even if a lot of my teammates aren't here. I like thinking of Ella getting close to my friends' partners and wives. I like the thought of her close, period.

Cam and Essence are at the big table with Banksy. Emerson Stag waves from beside Spinner, who appears to be explaining the rules of hockey to Aarthi using saltshakers. Mayhem occupies his usual corner, quietly watching the room fill.

Ella stands in the middle of it, and I watch her face cycle

through surprise, overwhelm, and then pure joy. These people are here for her. For Ella Rujkowski, RN.

Gianna emerges from the kitchen carrying a platter of red, steaming balls. "Mercy Balls," she announces, setting them down at the center of the table. "Meatballs in a Bloody Mary reduction with horseradish and celery salt. In honor of our girl and her new gig."

"That's disgusting," Spinner says, reaching for one. I notice that he winks at Gianna, and she actually blushes.

"It's genius," Aarthi corrects, already eating. Her eyes close.

Ella beams, one hand on her chest like she's trying to contain her heart from swelling out of her body. She pops a meatball in her mouth and moans. "Oh my god, Gianna."

I adjust my pants, reminding myself that we are here for my girl, and try one of the meatballs.

Gianna pats Ella's shoulder. "Eat. You're too skinny."

"Okay, boomer," Ella laughs at the restaurant owner who is the same age as me and Rookie.

"You're perfect," Gianna says, wiping her hands on her apron. "Please come often."

Spinner, incapable of passing on a joke, speaks with his mouth full. "That's what she said." He punches my shoulder just as Rookie pokes his head in the door and silently grabs a table. Ella hasn't seen him yet, so I focus on her as the room settles into the white noise of a raucous celebration.

Overlapping conversations, laughter, and the clink of glasses punctuate the party while McKenzie and Aarthi continue telling everyone how awesome Ella is at her job.

Ella tries to downplay it, and Essence shuts that down with a pointed "girl, take the compliment."

Ella is animated, hands moving, laughing, and I lean against the wall and watch her be a person people want to know. Not because of her last name. Because of her.

Spinner drops onto the bench beside me. "Nice shiner."

"Thanks."

"Rookie, do that?"

"Yep."

"You hit him back?"

"Nope."

Spinner nods slowly, processing this. "That was probably the right call."

"Probably."

He bumps my shoulder. "She's good for you, man. You're different."

"Different how?"

"You're … calmer." He gestures at the room. "You planned this. You got everyone together. That's always been your thing. But this time it's not about the party. It's about her." He takes a sip of his beer. "That's different."

I don't know what to say to that, so I just nod. Spinner claps my back and heads off to refill his drink.

Mayhem materializes beside me. He stands next to me against the wall and surveys the room. "You good?" he asks.

"Getting there."

He nods. Sips. Gestures his head toward Rookie, who is quietly eating, biding his time. That's the whole conversation. It's enough.

The door to the back room opens, and Grentley walks in.

This alone is unusual. Although I guess he's been coming out a little bit now that he finished anger management therapy or whatever went on with him and the Stag twins.

But tonight, Grentley walks in and scans the room until he finds Ella. He crosses directly to her, bypassing Spinner, ignoring Banksy's greeting, sidestepping McKenzie like she's a traffic cone. He stops in front of Ella, who looks up at him with the mild alarm at approached by a six-foot-two block of ice.

"Hi," she says. "Do you want a Mercy Ball?"

He shakes his head. "I heard you passed your nursing exam."

"I did."

He's quiet for a beat. "Thank you for doing that." The table around them goes still because Grentley voluntarily speaking to someone is an event. Then he says, "When I was seven, I broke my collarbone. The...adults...in charge of me didn't take me to the hospital for two days. When they finally brought me in, it was an ER nurse who figured out what was going on. She's the one who called protective services. She sat with me the whole time and told me I was brave."

The room is dead silent.

"I don't remember her name," Grentley continues, like he's casually discussing a hockey game. "But she changed my life. You're going to matter to people like that, Ella. Congratulations."

He turns, walks to the counter, picks up a tray Gianna has already prepared for him, and takes it to the corner without another word.

I stare at him. I've played with Josh Grentley for years. I've seen him block shots with his face, stare down charging forwards, shut out entire offenses without flinching. I have never once heard him volunteer personal information. Not in the locker room, not on road trips, not after wins or losses or anything in between.

He didn't even talk to us about his divorce. And now he just bared his soul in front of the team and the PAWs.

Ella's eyes are bright. She blinks, swallows, and pops another meatball in her mouth.

I'm about to sit down with her and finally relax when Rookie crosses the room to stand behind Ella. His eyes are red. His hair is worse than usual. Which makes sense since he's been driving around all day, probably confronting the possibility that he drove his sister away.

Ella turns from the table and looks up at her brother. For

once, he doesn't call her names or say something dumb. He squats down and wraps his arms around her, clinging like tape on the blade of a hockey stick.

Ella's hands come up to his back. She grips his hoodie, and I see her knuckles go white.

"I'm proud of you," Rookie says. His voice is thick and muffled against her hair. "I'm so proud of you, Ell."

She nods against his chest. Doesn't speak. Doesn't need to.

He holds her for a long time. Nobody cracks a joke. Nobody fills the silence. Even Spinner keeps his mouth shut, which might be the most remarkable event of the year. The whole thing, Grentley spewing his soul...Rookie feeling a feeling...it all has me thinking about my shitty dad and his own awful treatment of me. All the people in my life are here doing brave things, being vulnerable with their feelings and holding each other up.

Makes me want to *only* let in people who do the same to me.

When Rookie releases his sister, he turns and finds me against the wall. We look at each other, and I can see the calculations, the anger still there, but banked, covered by something more urgent. Gratitude, maybe. Or just the recognition that I found his sister when he couldn't.

He crosses to me and puts a hand on my back. Pats once. Firm. The way you'd tap a teammate's helmet after a good shift.

It's not forgiveness. But it's a start.

"Nice shiner," he says.

"You should see the other guy."

His mouth twitches. Almost a smile. Not quite. He drops his hand and walks to the table, where Gianna is already setting a plate in front of the empty seat she kept for him.

I lean against the wall and watch the Rujkowski siblings eat meatballs across from each other, and I know they're going to be okay. I soak it all in and think about what I can change, too. Other than being more openly with the woman I love.

Ella's hand reaches for the empty place beside her on the bench and glances up at me. My body and all my instincts scream at me to join her, to sit beside her, drape an arm over her shoulder. But I don't want to take away from her celebration here by stirring up more shit with her brother before we've had a chance to talk things out.

I hesitate while she continues to glance over at me, at the space beside her. And finally, Rookie groans and stares at the ceiling. "Just fucking sit with my sister, Howie."

CHAPTER 25
ELLA

Bernard slides onto the bench beside me, and his thigh presses against mine, and I feel my brother's eyes track the shift in Bernard's body. But Jason doesn't say anything. He eats a Mercy Ball and stares at the table, and I can see him working through something, the gears turning behind his bloodshot eyes.

The party continues around us — Aarthi is deep in conversation with Essence about healthcare policy, Gianna keeps bringing food — but our corner of the table has gone quiet. The three of us in our own pocket of gravity.

"So," Jason says.

"So," I say.

Bernard says nothing.

Jason pushes a meatball around his plate. "How long has this been going on for real?"

I glance at Bernard. He gives me the smallest nod. My story to tell.

"Since a few weeks after I moved in." I don't offer details. Jason doesn't need a timeline of sexual milestones. "It started as something … casual. And then it wasn't."

Jason looks at Bernard. "You tried casual with my sister?"

Bernard holds my brother's gaze. "No," he says. "Not really."

Jason eats another meatball. I watch him chew, and I think about all the meals I've eaten in the background of Jason's life: in arena parking lots, at team dinners where nobody asked my opinion, at family tables where the conversation revolved around his stats. This meal is different. He's listening. And eating food named in my honor.

"I owe you an apology," Jason says, and he's looking at me. "Not just for yesterday. For … a lot of stuff."

"Jason—"

"Let me get this out." He sets down his fork. "I didn't know you were unhappy. Growing up, I mean. I didn't realize you felt like you were just … along for the ride. I thought we were having fun."

"You were having fun. You were the one playing."

He winces. "Yeah. I'm getting that now." He rubs the back of his neck, a gesture so similar to Bernard's that I almost laugh. "I should have been better. I should have noticed."

"You're noticing now. That counts."

He nods. Picks his fork back up. Sets it down again. "I want to do something. And I need you to not argue with me about it."

"That's a big ask, bruh."

He grins and gestures at me with his fork. "There are units for sale in our building." He pauses to chew and swallow. "I want to buy you your own place. So you have a home that's actually yours."

I stare at him, not comprehending that he wants to *buy* me a condo. "Jason, that's—"

"I said don't argue."

"It's too much."

"It's not enough." His voice is rough. "I'm a freaking millionaire, and you had to take out loans for college, and then I didn't come through with my promise to help you land on your feet in a new city." He pushes his plate around with one hand, fidgeting. "Let me do this, Ella. I've got more money than I know what to do with, and my sister has been living out of a suitcase in my roommate's bedroom. Please let me buy you an apartment."

I look at Bernard, who is studying his plate with great intensity, clearly determined not to influence this conversation.

"Okay," I say. "Thank you."

Jason exhales. "Good. Okay." He picks up his fork and points it at Bernard. "And you."

Bernard raises his head.

"What I said in the parking lot. About your dad." Jason's jaw tightens. "That was a low blow. You're nothing like him, and I know that. I was pissed, and I went for the worst thing I could think of, and it wasn't fair."

Bernard nods slowly. "I appreciate that."

"I'm not saying I'm cool with all of this yet." Jason waves his fork between us. "But I'm trying."

"That's all I'm asking," Bernard says.

I reach under the table and take Bernard's hand. He threads his fingers through mine. Jason sees, and his face cycles through about four expressions before landing on resigned acceptance.

"Of course you fell for him," Jason mutters, stabbing a meatball. "It had to be a hockey guy."

"You have awesome taste in friends," I say. "That's really all this is."

Jason chews. Considers. "I can live with that."

The tension at our end of the table eases, and Bernard's thumb traces circles on my palm under the table. I press my knee harder against his thigh.

We eat. We talk. The weight of our secrets falls away, and I feel light.

After a while, I catch Bernard's eye and hold it, craving warmth that has nothing to do with meatball sauce.

"I think we're going to head out," Bernard says, pushing back from the table.

Jason looks at us. At our linked hands. At the way I'm leaning into Bernard's shoulder. "Fine." He waves us off. "Just don't be gross and suck face where I can see."

Bernard grins. "Is that a fourth rule? I'm losing track."

"Get out of here, Howie."

"Yes, sir." Bernard stands, pulls me up beside him, and grabs my coat from the back of the bench.

Jason watches us head for the door and calls out, "I'm giving you a head start. I need to call my realtor and my money guy."

"Thank you, Jason," I say from the doorway.

"Yeah, yeah." He's already on his phone. "Love you or whatever."

————

The cold hits us as we push through the front door. Bernard's arm settles around my shoulders, and I tuck against his side as we walk to the G-Wagon. I think about Bernard's hands and Bernard's mouth and the fact that we have an empty apartment waiting for us with no danger, no threat of failure in sight.

He starts the engine, and I watch his hands on the steering wheel, and I feel a surge of want so sharp it surprises me. This feeling is bold, sharp, and urgent. "Bernard."

"Yeah?"

"There's a lesson we never covered."

He glances at me. "What?"

I trail my fingers along the center console. "Car sex."

The G-Wagon swerves. Bernard's knuckles go white on the wheel. "Ella."

"This car has a very spacious back seat."

"We are not—I'm not—this is a moving vehicle."

"I'm just saying. For future reference." I run my palm slowly across my chest, tracing the neckline of my sweater, and watch his eyes dart from the road to my hand and back. "The leather is very nice."

"Ella Rujkowski, I am operating heavy machinery."

"Noted." I reach across the console and rest my hand on his thigh. His quad tenses under my palm, and I hear his breath catch, and I feel powerful in a way that has become familiar and addictive. "I can wait until we get back to the condo."

"Thank you."

"But I'm very, very turned on right now."

He drives faster. I leave my hand on his thigh and watch Pittsburgh blur past the window, and I think about the first time I sat in this passenger seat, freezing, annoyed, on my way from the airport to crash on a couch. Bernard was a stranger then. A childhood annoyance with bloodshot eyes and a hat pulled low.

Now his leg is warm under my hand, and his jaw is tight with desire, and he's driving me to the place where we figured each other out over meatballs and medical quizzes and gentle, luxurious touches.

"Bernard?"

"If you say car sex again, I'll wreck."

"I was going to say I love you."

The car goes quiet. His hand leaves the wheel and covers mine on his thigh. He squeezes once. Twice.

"I love you too, Ella." His voice is rough and certain. "I've loved you for so long and been afraid of how I feel."

He lifts my hand and kisses my knuckles without taking his eyes off the road. My own eyes fill with tears. I'm so happy right now, joyful in a way I never even imagined. This man beside me helped me grab the career I'm good at, and I love him. And he loves me back. It's surreal, and yet … here he is. Real. Solid. Mine.

I lace my fingers through his and hold on for the rest of the drive.

PLANCHET BROOKE   182

man beside me helped me prepare the meal. I'm good at and
love him, and he takes me back. It's magical, and you... her
by a knock, cold. Mmm.

I bet my sugar's through the ... and hold on for the rest of
the time.

CHAPTER 26
HOWIE

Horny Ella is really freaking hot.

She kicks off her shoes in the entryway, and I press her against the wall and kiss her the way I've wanted to for months. I kiss her with my whole body, both hands in her hair, nothing held back, and nobody to hide from. She grabs my shirt and pulls me closer and moans my name, and I feel it vibrate through my chest.

We stumble down the hall, shedding layers as we go. Her sweater lands on the floor. My shirt catches on a doorknob. She's laughing and kissing me at the same time, and the combination is the best thing I've ever tasted.

We fall through the bedroom door, and I walk her backward until her legs hit the mattress. She sits on the edge and looks up at me, and her face in the lamplight is everything I almost lost.

"I love you," I tell her, because I can say it now, because it's true. Because I spent weeks choking on it, and I refuse to waste another second. "I love you, Ella."

Her eyes go bright. "I love you too."

I exhale a cloud of joy at her words, relief flooding my body alongside a deep desire to please her. "Good," I grunt. "Now let me show you."

I drop to my knees without a whisper of pain. Weeks of rehab, PT, ice rotations, and compression wraps, and my knee is fine. It's perfect. It works exactly the way it's supposed to, which means I can kneel in front of Ella Rujkowski and do what I've been desperate to do since the first time I saw her at the airport.

I hook my fingers in the waistband of her jeans. She lifts her hips, and I pull them down, along with her underwear, and she's bare from the waist down, sitting on the edge of my bed, and with me between her thighs.

"Bernard." Her voice is breathy. "What is this—ohh."

"I need to taste you." I press my mouth to the inside of her knee. Her leg trembles. "I have wanted this since before I had any right to want it. Please let me."

She nods. Her hand finds my hair. I kiss the inside of her thigh, slow, deliberate, working my way up. She falls back on her elbows and watches me with dark eyes and parted lips, and I take my time because this matters. This is the "lesson" I never gave her, the one I kept putting off because I knew — I knew — that once I put my mouth on her I wouldn't be able to pretend this was tutoring.

The first taste of her shuts down every higher function in my brain. I grip her thighs and pull her closer to the edge of the bed, and I press my tongue flat against her clit, and she makes a sound that I want engraved on my headstone.

"Oh, my god." Her hand tightens in my hair. "Bernard… oh my god."

I learn what makes her gasp and grip me tighter. The place that makes her hips buck off the mattress and the rhythm that makes her voice climb. I use my mouth, and my tongue, and my hands, and I give her everything I've been holding back, every ounce of the want I stored up during weeks of secret couch sessions and careful car rides and the aching discipline of sleeping on the other side of a wall.

"I love you," she gasps, and her back arches and her thick

thighs clamp around my ears, and I can barely hear her, but I feel the words in the flex of her body. "I love you, Bernard, I love — oh, fuck — I love—"

She comes against my mouth, and I hold her through it, hands on her hips, lips on her skin, feeling her pulse and contract and shake apart. I don't stop until she pushes at my head, oversensitive, laughing, and panting.

"Get up here," she says. "Please. I need you."

I climb off the floor and onto the bed, covering her body with mine. She pulls my face down and kisses me, and I know she can taste herself on my mouth, and the groan she makes tells me she doesn't mind. Her hands work my belt, my zipper, shoving my jeans down while I kick them off the rest of the way.

I reach for the nightstand, but she puts a hand on my arm. "I had a checkup," she tells me, "for work. And I asked to get on the pill."

I freeze, a condom packet in my hand, trying to understand the meaning of her words. "What are you telling me, baby?"

Ella licks her lower lip, staring at my hand, then at my crotch. "I'm healthy, and I can't get pregnant. And I want to feel you. All of you. Inside me."

"Bare?" The thought sends a surge of need through my lower half. Can I even handle the idea of sliding inside Ella with no barriers, nothing between us? Fuck, I want to try and find out.

"Bare. Yes, please." She drizzles lube from a packet, and her slick hand wraps around me, and I drop my forehead to her shoulder and groan. "Ella."

"I love you," she says, guiding me. "I love you, and I want you inside me."

I press into her, naked and throbbing, and we both exhale, forehead to forehead, breathing each other's air. The fullness of being inside Ella. The heat, the pressure, the feeling of her body opening for mine, never gets less over-whelming. Every time feels like the first time in the ways that matter: the shock of connection, the certainty that this is where I belong.

"Move," she whispers. "Please."

I move. Slow at first because I want to feel everything. Her hips meeting mine. Her hands on my back. The sounds she makes directly into my ear. "I've never done this, Ella, never."

I feel every bit of her body, the way she clings to me, the way her pussy is made for my cock. Her legs wrap around my waist, and her heels dig into my ass, and I bury my face in her neck and breathe her in.

"You're everything," I tell her. "You know that? Everything."

She pulls my face up so she can see me. Her eyes are wet, but she's smiling, and the combination wrecks me. "You're my person, Bernard."

"I'm your what?"

"My big, ridiculous St. Bernard."

I laugh, which changes the angle, which makes her gasp, which makes me thrust harder. The rhythm builds. Her nails drag down my back, and I feel the sting and love it. She grips my shoulders and holds on.

"Harder," she says, and I obey, because Ella Rujkowski knows what she wants and I will give her anything she asks for as long as I live.

The bed creaks. The headboard taps the wall. She's loud, and I'm louder, and I don't care that Jason could come home and hear us through the floor because we're done hiding. We're done with rules, secrets, and separate sleeping arrange-ments. This is us, in our room, making noise, taking up all the space we want.

"I'm close," she says. "Bernard — right there — don't stop—"

"I love you." I brace one arm beside her head and cup her

face with the other and watch her. "I love you, Ella. Come for me."

She does. Eyes open, locked on mine, and the sight of her face in the moment she lets go is the single most beautiful thing I will ever see. It pulls me over the edge with her. I come hard, burying myself deep, saying her name like it's the only word in any language that matters.

I feel myself spurting in her body, hot and wet, and I imagine that one day, she won't be on the pill, and this will be me making a baby with Ella. I see our forever together, and it sends another wave of release through my super-satisfied junk.

We lie in the wreckage of the bed, breathing hard, tangled up in each other and the sheets. Her head is on my chest. My hand is in her hair. The lamplight pools around us, and the room is warm and quiet and ours.

"Your knee is better," she murmurs.

"My knee is great."

"I noticed." She traces a circle on my chest.

I kiss the top of her head. "I'm going to want to do that again. Frequently. Possibly constantly."

She tilts her chin up and looks at me. Flushed, satisfied, hair a disaster, eyes soft. "We have time."

"Yeah?"

"I'm staying, Bernard. I'm staying in Pittsburgh, and I'm staying in the ER, and I'm staying with you."

I pull her closer. Press my face into her hair. Breathe.

"Good because I wasn't ever going to let you leave," I say, and I mean it in every way a person can mean it — this bed, this city, this life I didn't know I wanted until she walked through an airport and revealed herself as everything I always wanted.

CHAPTER 27
HOWIE

THERE'S NOTHING MORE COMFORTING THAN THE SMELL OF TAPE adhesive, rubber mats, and the rink stink of guys who push me beyond the limits of normal humans.

I've missed this, the ritual of it, the muscle memory of pulling on gear, the way the world narrows to a set of very simple instructions: skate, hit, shoot, win.

My knee bends clean as I squat to lace my skates. No pain. No hesitation.

"Dude!" Spinner shouts from across the room, stick-tapping the floor in my direction. "Our line is back."

"Miss me?"

"Like a rash." He grins. "You ready?"

"Born ready."

Cappy swings by my stall and claps my shoulder. "Good to have you back. Don't be stupid with that knee."

"When have I ever been stupid?"

"Do you want the full list or the highlights?"

Rookie is three stalls down, taping his stick. He catches my eye and nods. We've been okay. Not back to normal, not fully healed, but functional. I've been sleeping in my room with Ella the past few nights, and I get how that's probably weird for him.

Shouldn't be too much longer. He closed on Ella's new condo and will get the keys soon.

"Your girl's up with the PAWs," he says now, not looking up from his tape job.

"I know."

"Cam got her a jersey."

I pause mid-lace. "Whose jersey?"

Jason's mouth twitches. "Yours, dipshit."

Something warm spreads through my chest. Ella is in the family section wearing my jersey, not one with her own last name on it. Ella, who spent her childhood watching hockey from the margins, is sitting with the PAWs and cheering for me on purpose.

"Don't get all weepy," Spinner says. "Save it for the ice."

"Speaking of the ice." Mayhem appears, fully dressed, looking like a tank with shin pads. He settles on the bench beside me and says, in the tone of a man who has been waiting for the right moment, "Did you call Benny about the podcast thing?"

I pull my jersey over my head. "What about it?"

"The second interview. Your dad did another one."

My hands freeze on the hem. "What?"

"Yeah, man. Spinner's agent flagged it this morning." Mayhem watches my face. "Your agent didn't say anything?"

The locker room noise continues around us, but I feel a clench in my stomach. Another interview. Another podcast. My father is running his mouth on any microphone that'll have him, and my agent — the agent my father set me up with — is not even monitoring it.

"Why are you still with that guy?" Mayhem asks.

I don't have a good answer. The honest truth is that Benny came through my father's connections, another tie to the Houser name. But the Houser name has been doing me damage for twenty-six years, and maybe it's time I chose my own path.

Spinner drops onto the bench on my other side. "Brian Klein is here tonight. He's sitting with the Stags in the family section."

"Brian Klein?"

"My agent. The best agent." Spinner taps my chest with his stick. "I already told him about you. He wants to chat after the game."

"You told your agent about me?"

"I told him you're talented, underrepresented, and your current agent sucks balls." Spinner shrugs. "He's interested."

I look at Mayhem, who nods. Then the Stag twins chime in that this Brian guy is their agent, too. "He works miracles," Alder says. "And he'll get you endorsements."

Gunnar Stag, one of our rotating killer goalies, pounds me on the head with his fist. "Prepare for a milk mustache, guy."

I realize with sudden clarity that I've been overlooking a huge part of the career of a professional athlete. My friends all have branding deals that are flooding their bank accounts. I sort of figured Rookie fell into the meat advertisements, but listening to Gunnar talk about milk ads, I realize that agents actively make all this happen.

I've just been floating along here. Anger at my father starts to claw its way to the surface, but I need to save that for the ice, direct it where I can work it right out of my body.

"Okay," I say to Spinner instead. "I'll talk to your guy."

"Attaboy." Spinner hops up and gestures toward the door. "Now let's go beat Columbus."

Coach calls us in. We huddle, we break, and I follow the guys into the tunnel with my stick on the ice and my heart hammering and the noise of the arena building above us like a wave about to crest.

Standing just outside the door is a man, the Stag brothers and Spinner approach warmly, greeting him with fist bumps. I think this is their shared agent, the infamous Brian Klein.

The guy looks around Spinner and steps forward, hand

out. "Houser. These guys talk about you nonstop. Let's have a conversation after the game."

I shake his hand. "Yeah. I'd like that."

"Good." Brian pops his gum and grins. "I've got ideas for you, kid. Big ones."

He claps my shoulder the way you'd acknowledge a player after a good shift and walks past me toward the ice. I stare at him, realizing I might be an actual adult now, with a real agent who can help me get real money and look after me.

"Houser!" Coach's voice from down the tunnel interrupts my thoughts. "You playing tonight or sightseeing?"

I skate onto the ice.

The arena is loud and bright, and eighteen thousand people are on their feet, and the ice is fresh and perfect under my blades. I take warmup laps and feel my knee hold and my lungs open and my legs find the rhythm that I've known since I was four years old in a Minnesota rink with my dad's shadow over every stride.

But tonight the shadow is gone. Instead, with my girl in the stands and my name on her back and the weight of a secret lifted, I feel like every spotlight in this place is lighting my way.

The game starts fast. Columbus is physical, and we match them hit-for-hit. I play the second line with Spinner, cycling the puck, crashing the net, feeling the rust shake off with every shift. My timing is half a step behind, but my instincts are there — the reads, the angles, the sense of where the puck is going before it gets there.

Mayhem lays a guy out in the neutral zone, so clean that the arena roars. Rookie wins a faceoff and feeds it back to defense. Grentley makes a save that draws a standing ovation. The Stag twins work the power play like they share a brain.

Then I'm on the ice for a line change, fresh legs, and Spinner chips the puck along the wall. I chase it into the corner, shoulder down, muscle some defenseman off the biscuit — clean, hard, the way you're supposed to, not the way my father did it — and center it in front of the net.

It bounces off a skate. Comes back to me. I'm alone in the slot with the puck on my blade and the goalie sliding across, and I don't think. I just shoot.

Suddenly, the light goes red, the horn blows, and the arena explodes. Spinner crashes into me from behind, screaming in my ear, and the boys swarm me until I'm at the center of a hockey hug with my knee intact and my name on the scoreboard.

I peel myself away from the scrum and skate toward the bench, gloves up, stick raised, and I look up at the family section.

Ella is on her feet. She's in my jersey, and she's screaming, both fists in the air, and Cam is hugging her from one side and Essence from the other. My teammates' partners and parents are all together with my girl, whose face shows pure, incandescent joy.

She sees me looking. Our eyes lock through the glass, through the noise, through people, and the distance between the ice and the stands.

She points at me. Then she presses her hand against her heart.

I press my glove against mine.

CHAPTER 28
ELLA

I'VE SPENT MY WHOLE LIFE IN HOCKEY ARENAS, BUT ALWAYS IN the general seats. The cheap ones behind a pillar, the nosebleeds my dad scored through a booster club, the standing-room spots where I did homework on my knees while Jason's team warmed up below. I never sat with the families. I was adjacent to the families. Background noise in someone else's experience.

Tonight I'm in the third row behind the glass with a HOUSER jersey and the other guys' partners all around me. Cam and Essence are there, and Emerson Stag has a baby strapped to her chest, wearing tiny little headphones to block the incredible noise from the crowd and the speakers.

When the announcer calls Howie Houser's name, I feel it in my sternum. My heart stutters each time the puck drops. Cam drops a hand on my shoulder and squeezes. "It gets easier," he says, gesturing at the ice. "But I thought you'd be used to it with your brother and all."

I bite my lip, wondering how to explain that I somehow care a lot more about the man that I love getting injured. There's no way to verbalize that yet, so I just squeeze her hand each time a Fury player collides with the glass.

I watch a Columbus forward drive Jason into the boards,

and I realize I've barely watched him play since he went pro. It's different now, with my education on the human body and my experience with all the damage it can endure. I see the angle of impact on my brother's shoulder, and I calculate a rotator cuff strain and possible AC joint separation, and my hands grip the armrest.

"You okay?" Cam asks.

"Fine." But it's a total lie.

Bernard's first shift is forty-five seconds long. He skates hard, cycles the puck, takes a clean hit along the wall, and comes off for a line change. I don't breathe until he's on the bench.

Essence squeezes my arm again. "You learn to trust the pads."

"I've seen what the pads don't cover."

She laughs. "Fair. But your man is tough."

My man. I watch Bernard on the bench, drinking water, listening to Coach, and I think: *my man*. The words fit in a way I didn't expect.

Jason wins a faceoff in the second period, and I surprise myself by cheering. Not the obligatory clap of a sister who was dragged along — a real, involuntary shout that makes Cam look at me with raised eyebrows.

I've spent twenty-three years resenting my brother's sport for consuming every resource my family had. But watching Jason now, seeing his speed, his instinct, the way he reads the ice, I realize he's good at this. And being proud of him doesn't diminish me the way I always thought it would. There's room for both.

Then Bernard hops over the boards for a fresh shift, and I forget about my brother entirely.

My boyfriend scores a freaking goal, and suddenly I'm screaming like a deranged fan, both fists in the air. I find myself wishing I was out there in the pile of guys congratulating him, but then he's skating toward our section and looking up. For me, I realize.

Our eyes meet through the glass, and I feel a swell of pride, connection, and contentment. I point at him and press my hand to my heart to convey what I'm feeling.

He presses his glove to his.

The arena roars around us, but I don't notice. I'm basking in the wonder of choosing this place, this man, this life. This isn't something secondhand or the scraps of someone else's success. This is mine.

The Fury wins 4-2, and the crowd erupts. Cam grabs my hand, and he pulls me toward the corridor where the families wait for players to emerge from the locker room.

Other partners cluster in groups. Some with kids, some dressed up, all carrying the particular energy of folks who love men who do violent things for a living and then come home tender.

After an eternity, the locker room door opens, and players filter out in postgame suits with wet hair and flushed faces. Spinner emerges first, scanning the hallway until he spots our group. "PAWs. Who's buying drinks?"

"Not me," Cam says. "I bought last time."

"That was November."

"And I'm still recovering." He shakes his head before finding his husband and pulling Banksy in for a kiss.

Jason comes out next, suit jacket over one arm, and gives me a nod that contains approximately forty percent less hostility than it would have a week ago. Progress.

Then Bernard walks through the door, and every coherent thought in my head evaporates.

He's in a charcoal suit with no tie, top button undone, hair still damp and curling at his temples. His black eye has faded to a greenish yellow that somehow makes him look more attractive, not less. He scans the hallway the way he scanned the airport baggage claim two months ago, except this time, when his eyes find me, he doesn't have to pretend he's not looking.

"There's my girl," he says, and his arms open, and I walk into them and press my face against his chest and breathe in soap and ice and Bernard.

"Great game," I murmur into his shirt.

"Great jersey." His hand finds the nameplate on my back and traces it through the fabric. "Looks good on you."

Somewhere behind us, Spinner is organizing a group outing. A bar, apparently, where the whole team can celebrate the win. Cam and Essence are in. The Stag brothers are discussing logistics and babysitters. Jason is on his phone, presumably coordinating something that involves protein.

Bernard looks down at me. "You want to go out?"

I look up at him. "I want to go home."

His eyes darken. His hand tightens on my back. "Yeah?"

"Take me home, Bernard."

We say our goodbyes. Spinner calls us boring. Cam gives me a knowing look. Jason watches us leave and says nothing, which at this point qualifies as enthusiastic support.

The parking garage is cold and dim and mostly empty — the fans cleared out during the locker room wait, and the concrete cavern echoes with our footsteps. Bernard's G-Wagon is parked in the players' section, tucked in a far corner near the wall.

He clicks the key fob. The lights flash. I grab his hand and pull him past the driver's door, toward the back of the car.

He arches a brow. "Ella?"

"There are still things I haven't tried, Bernard." I open the rear door. The leather interior glows in the overhead light, wide and deep and private. "Care to teach me about car sex finally?"

He stares at me. Then, in the back seat. Then, at the empty garage around us. "We're in public."

"A very dark, very empty parking structure." I climb in

and sit on the leather and look at him standing outside, jaw working, hands clenching, visibly losing the battle between responsibility and desire. I unzip my pants and wiggle them down around my ankles. "Are you coming?"

His eyes blaze as he leaps in, closing the door. The overhead light fades, and we're in darkness with our feelings and our pulsing sexual tension.

"I love you," I tell him, pulling his face to mine. "I love you, and I'm so proud of you, and I want you right here."

"I love you too," he says against my mouth. "I love you, and this is a terrible idea, and I'm absolutely going to give you what you need."

He maneuvers us so I'm on my knees on the back seat, with him behind me running his hands long his name on my spine, cupping my ass, sliding into me bare and hot and hard with his suit barely undone.

We laugh and fumble and thrust, grunting together in the dark, and it's not graceful. It's messy and perfect and so fucking hot I come twice before Bernard is pressing into me, groaning in release.

"I can't believe you talked me into car sex," he murmurs against my neck.

"I can't believe it took this long."

He pulls out, shaking his head, reaching for napkins from the console to wipe up the mess he left between my legs. "Ella, we've only been together for two months."

I let my knees fall open while he cleans me up, appreciating everything about this. "You've been an incredible tutor."

He rears back to look at me, his face barely visible in the dark, lit only by the glow of the garage exit sign. "I'm not your tutor anymore."

"No." I trace his eyebrow scar with my thumb. "You're my person."

"Your big, slobbery St. Bernard."

"Who rescued me?"

"You rescued yourself, Ella." He kisses my forehead. "I just drove the car."

I pull him closer, and we stop talking for a while. The G-Wagon's windows fog in the cold garage air, and the leather seat is warm beneath us, and I feel Bernard's hands and Bernard's mouth. This man who showed up every single time I needed him, and most of the times I said I didn't, whispers to me how he wants to cut ties with his father. How he met a new agent and learned the phrase 'cease and desist.'

We lie tangled in the back seat, my head on his chest, his hand tracing slow circles on my hip. The parking garage is silent except for the tick of the cooling engine and the distant hum of the arena above, and my boyfriend telling me all his troubles and his plans to overcome them.

I settle against his chest and close my eyes and listen to his heartbeat and feel absolutely, completely, ridiculously whole.

HOWIE

ONE MONTH LATER

ELLA'S PLACE IS TWO FLOORS BELOW JASON'S, BUT IT FEELS LIKE A different world entirely.

She got the keys and, thanks to McKenzie and Aarthi, started thrifting and gathering all the furniture and decorations I'd expect to see in a movie depiction of the perfect girl pad.

Everything here feels soft and cozy, and I am frankly jittery with excitement at sleeping here. As soon as she gets a bed.

Today, the Fury has an off day, so the guys and I are all here helping her get settled—putting together IKEA furniture, hanging art, and all the stuff she might need tall guys to help with.

I stand in the living room with a power drill and a curtain rod while Spinner and Rookie argue over their interpretation of the instructions for assembling Ella's bookshelf.

Mayhem is silent in the kitchen, unpacking glassware, handling each Thatcher Stag original piece as if it were a work of art. He and Ella are probably the only people I know who could casually use actual designer cups and not worry about breaking them.

Suddenly, Rookie shrieks in the process of unpacking books for the new shelves. "Dude," I hold my ear. "What is your problem?"

Rookie waves a book around. "What is this? Why is my baby sister reading this?"

I squint and notice a shirtless man on the cover of the book, and, glancing in the box, it's not the only romance novel she had shipped here from Minnesota.

Ella walks into the room, hands on her hips, and frowns at him. "Jason Rujkowski. Did I question the violent murder videogames in your home? I thank you for keeping your opinions to yourself."

She plucks the book from his hands, clutches it to her chest, and then sets it on her shelf in pride of place.

McKenzie and Aarthi emerge from where they're stocking the bathroom, helping themselves to a few oohs and aahs over Ella's book collection.

While Rookie grumbles, I finish hanging the curtains. My girl needs privacy for when she's reading her naked-man books ... or doing other things in her living room.

She smiles, and I see it, the recognition of what I'm doing. I lift the rod into the brackets, and the dark gray fabric falls straight and even, and the room transforms.

"Perfect," she says.

"I know."

Spinner starts organizing a lunch order when Mayhem's phone buzzes on the kitchen counter. He glances at the screen, and something happens to his face. I've seen Mayhem take a cross-check to the spine without flinching, but whatever is on that screen makes him go pale.

He sets down the Allen wrench, stares at his phone, and his jaw works in a way I've never seen from him, like something cracked in his skull.

"Mayhem?" I set down the drill. "You good?"

He looks up. His eyes are wrong. "I have to go."

Spinner snorts. "You chasing a lady friend, Mayhem?" Our friend glares at Spinner, who holds his hands up in supplication. "Sorry. What's actually wrong?"

"I just… I need to handle something." He's already grabbing his jacket from the back of a chair, moving fast. All of us —Rookie, Spinner, McKenzie, Aarthi, and Ella—stare at him in disbelief. Mayhem doesn't bolt from a room like the floor is on fire.

We all watch Mayhem shove his feet into his shoes and reach for the door.

"Cameron," I say, dropping his real name to convey the gravity of whatever is going on. "Talk to me."

He pauses with his hand on the knob and seems to get his shit together, because when he turns, his face is composed again. "I'm fine," he says. "Congratulations on the place, Ella."

And then he's gone. The door clicks shut, and his footsteps echo down the hallway, and the rest of us stand in Ella's half-assembled apartment in silence.

"What the hell was that?" Spinner asks.

Rookie shakes his head. "I've never seen him move that fast off the ice."

Spinner licks his teeth, then asks, "Should we go after him?"

"No," I say, though it goes against every instinct I have. "And quit bugging him about ladies." Mayhem let slip the other day that he's been seeing the team psychologist, so something is definitely up with him. "He'll come to us when he's ready."

I don't know if that's true, but I know that chasing Mayhem when he doesn't want to be found is like chasing a puck into the corner against a guy twice your size. You'll just bounce off.

Spinner and Jason exchange a look. The energy in the room has shifted. The easy moving-day banter replaced by the quiet concern of men who love their friend and don't know what to do about it.

Ella breaks the silence. "Okay. Everyone out."

Spinner blinks. "What?"

"Out. Go home. I love you all, but I need to be alone in my apartment for ten minutes." She herds Spinner toward the door with the authority of a charge nurse clearing a trauma bay. "Go eat your meatballs. And thank you. Truly."

"You sure?" Jason asks from the doorway.

"I'm sure. Thank you for today. All of you." She hugs her brother and each of the girls. I reach for my jacket as everyone heads to the hall toward the elevator.

"Not you," Ella says.

I set the jacket down.

She closes the door, turns to me, leans against it, and we stand in her living room looking at each other.

"Hi," she says.

"Hi?"

She pushes off the door, crosses the room to me, and puts her hands on my chest. I cover them with mine. Her ring finger is bare, but I can picture something there, someday, and the thought doesn't scare me the way it would have three months ago. In fact, it turns me on.

"I bought a really nice bed," she says. "With my first real paycheck."

"I heard. California king."

"It won't be here until next week."

"That's a shame."

"It is." She slides her hands up my chest to my shoulders. "We'll just have to make do."

I look at the floor. The rug Aarthi helped her pick — soft, thick, big enough for two people who don't mind being close.

The late-afternoon sun hits it through the gap between the curtains, and it glows.

I like what my girl is thinking.

I pull my shirt over my head as Ella strips, and we sink together onto the rug, tangled in each other. She smells a little sweaty and a whole lot mine as I lay her back and hover over her curves.

Through it all, she looks up at me with those sharp, steady eyes. "I love you, Bernard."

"I love you, Ella."

I make love to her on the floor, slow and unhurried, sweet and so very good, because there's no one to hide from and nowhere to be.

Her hands grip my shoulders. My mouth finds her neck, her collarbone—anywhere I can paint with kisses. She wraps those solid legs around me and pulls me deeper into her and says my name, and I say hers, and we move together in the way we've learned, the way our bodies figured out before our brains caught up.

"I love you," she says again when she's close.

"I love you," I say when I feel her tighten around me.

"I love you," we repeat together, and I bury my face in her hair and let go.

We lie on the rug in the quiet. Her head on my chest. My hand in her hair. The curtains filter the river light to a warm gray, and the room smells like new paint, cardboard, and us.

Ella traces a circle on my stomach. "You gonna check on Mayhem?"

"Tomorrow," I tell her. And then I roll her on top of me, smiling as her hair falls around us in a silken curtain. "Tonight you're mine."

She hums against my chest. Content. Whole. Home.

Ready to see what has Mayhem so upset? Grab Playing it

Safe to fall in love with him and BB—a defender on the Pittsburgh Uprising women's hockey team.

Want a sneak peek into Howie and Ella's happily ever after? My newsletter subscribers can read a super cute bonus scene where Howie plans a really cute date. Visit www.LaineyDavis.com or scan the QR code below.

AUTHOR'S NOTE

I worked on this book in the first quarter of 2026, and it's hard to explain how tumultuous life was during that time. I had to take the city bus to the emergency room during a blizzard, where I was admitted for a liver infection caused by my faulty gall bladder. While I was in there, my roof got an ice dam, and my youngest child got head lice.

It. Was. A. Mess.

But I had a whole community of people helping my family—delivering meals, running errands, lending us Subarus when the city took an entire week to plow out the blizzard's snow deposits.

Through it all, writing this book was my escape. I spent a lot of time imagining these characters, dreaming about them at night, listening to them shout at me. I hope you like what they decided their story would be.

All my Playing book covers have been created by the incredible team at Qamber Designs, a boutique firm based in Bahrain. I mention this because while everything was happening with my personal guts, the world around my artist friends was literally on fire as bombs fell and bullets tore through the peace. I wasn't sure if my longtime collaborators were safe. They weren't sure, either. But they said work was their own escape from the madness, and I love the cover they made for Bernard and Ella.

Romance novels are such an escape for me, writing and reading them. And I know this is true for many others. I hope this book brings you some comfort during a time when the world is very scary for so many.

Purchasing this book helps provide paid work for a lot of human beings, including my cover designer, my editors, my narrators, my audio engineer, and my GI surgeon, who got me back on my feet by the equinox. Thank you for reading and supporting the team.

Many thanks belong to Elizabeth Perry, who always reads my shitty first drafts, and to Steph for providing all the nursing intel. And thank you to my beloved husband, who shaved the heads of our lousy offspring while I was in the hospital, in between emptying buckets of roof water.

ALSO BY LAINEY DAVIS

The Playing Series Hockey Romance

Playing for Keeps (Gunnar and Emerson)

Playing for Payback (Alder and Lena)

Playing with Fire (Tucker and Sloane)

Lit for Him (Brian and Noa)

Playing with Trouble (Howie and Ella)

Playing it Safe (Mayhem and BB)